Also by M.L. Joslyn
From Indigo Sea Press

Try Me On

indigoseapress.com

Subject X

By

M.L. Joslyn

Bramble Patch Books
Published by Indigo Sea Press
Winston-Salem

Bramble Patch Books
Indigo Sea Press
302 Ricks Drive
Winston-Salem, NC 27103

Copyright 2016 by M.L. Joslyn
First Bramble Patch Books edition published
March, 2016
Bramble Patch Books, Moon Sailor and all production design are trademarks of Indigo Sea Press, used under license.

For information regarding bulk purchases of this book, digital purchase and special discounts, please contact the publisher at indigoseapress@gmail.com

Cover design by Pan Morelli
Manufactured in the United States of America
ISBN 978-1-63066-292-9

Chapter One

"Describe what you see in this photograph. Can you do that?"

"The picture's pretty clear, isn't it? I mean, I'm not naïve, if that's what you're wondering."

"Amy, this is important. We have to establish a baseline for your responses. Please describe what you see."

"What sort of test is this? What is it you want to know—how broken I am?"

"This isn't a therapy session, Amy. We're not interested in fixing you—if, in fact, you are in need of fixing." Brooke spoke clearly but with zero emotion. Her legs were crossed, clenched in a statement of polished professionalism, or perhaps anxiety.

Brooke glanced at Jeremy, who sat to her right in a featureless, burgundy-colored club chair, his pale blue eyes locked on the girl seated across from them. She wasn't sure if they were on the same wavelength regarding Amy. This was their first study together, and she was struggling to read his thoughts.

From the other side of the squat, cherry wood coffee table, Amy peered back at her interviewers, wondering what she'd gotten herself into. One afternoon, a few questions, a hundred bucks. She had the time and she needed the money, so it seemed like a no-brainer. Now she wished she had asked a few qualifying questions herself.

"It's a picture of four people, four naked people. Is that enough detail?" As Amy's words scuffled from her mouth, her eyes wandered past the disquieted man and woman and settled on the unadventurous panel of biscuit-hued wallpaper behind them.

Jeremy glanced at Brooke and gestured toward the door.

1

"Excuse us for a minute, Amy." Jeremy rose from his chair and marched from the room, Brooke on his heels. They huddled in the quiet hallway, waiting for the crisp snap of the latching door.

"She's cold, Brooke. We're not going to get what we need from her."

"Well, she's ours for the afternoon, and we don't have anyone else scheduled until Tuesday. Maybe she'll loosen up."

"This study is important to me—to you—to us. We should have been more careful, spent more time selecting the respondents."

"We can make this work, Jeremy. It's going to take us forever to collect our responses. It's going to take even longer to evaluate them and write our papers. We need her."

"Alright, alright. Maybe she's just a little nervous. Let's go back in. But let me ask the first couple of questions. You might have come across as a bit adversarial. You know, a little too protective of your nest. When one female tries to...."

"Jeremy, I'm about to receive my doctorate in human sexual behavior. I know a couple of things—please."

"Sorry. Bad habit of mine, I guess. Let's get back in there before she sneaks out the window."

Amy stared patiently at the door, waiting for it to open. It was nothing more than a heavy slab of excessively varnished wood, interrupted by a straightforward brass knob. Closed, it provided a certain assurance of security—unwarranted, yet impressive. It also promised muted conversations; whatever was spoken in the room stayed in the room. And whatever was spoken in the hallway, well, Amy hadn't heard a damn word.

She knew the reason they had left the room was to talk about her. Otherwise, why would they have bothered? She didn't really care what they had to say. She just wanted the cash. Easy money, she had thought—an afternoon of breezy questions that called for candid answers—that's all. She wouldn't be judged, and she wouldn't be required to explain herself. At least that's the way Brooke explained it when she had solicited her outside Denney Hall after sociology class.

"My apologies, Amy. Brooke and I needed to discuss a couple of things. You're the first of twenty interviews we're conducting, but I don't want you to think we're not fully prepared."

"Hey, you have to start with someone."

"Yes. Yes, we do. Listen, Amy, I'm going to turn the recorder back on now, okay? Are you comfortable with that? Is there anything I can get you? Some more tea, perhaps? Is the room too bright, too dim? Hmm?"

"I'm very comfortable, thank you. What is it I've done anyway? You showed me a photograph of some people, nude people, and I told you what I saw. I'm not sure I understand your expectations of me."

"Brooke and I expect you to be yourself, that's all. But don't hold back, Amy. Okay? We're ready to listen to what you have to say. It doesn't matter how you respond to our questions—as long as you're honest with us."

"It's lust, I think."

"I'm sorry?"

"The photograph. It's lust. That's what I see."

Amy tried to read the faces of the man and woman sitting across from her. Had she supplied them with a satisfactory answer? Her gut told her no, they were looking for something else. But they had asked for an honest answer, and that's what she had given them.

"That's good, Amy. You see beyond the veneer. Keep going."

3

"Keep going?"

"Yes, please." Brooke flashed an easy smile Amy's way. The only thing left for Amy to tell them was what anyone could tell them. They didn't need her for that. There was no need for them to have loitered about the social sciences building enlisting survey takers. They should've just recruited agriculture students. "I see one woman and three men. The woman has shoulder- length auburn hair, narrow hips and looks to be fairly toned—nice arms, strong legs. I can't really see her face since she's bent over; her hair is in the way. If I had to guess, I'd bet she's very pretty. She's blowing the guy beneath her—the guy who's lying on the floor with his arms stretched to his sides, as if the last thing he wants to do is touch the woman. He seems more than naked somehow; he's not even wearing an expression. I suppose I could describe him …further."

"Tell us what you see—please."

"I can't really see his penis or much of it. The part that's not in the woman's mouth is pretty thick. I could only guess that it's long as well, based on her expression. She looks …stuffed. I think she's taken him as deep as she can. The other two men, I'm not sure what to make of them. They might be into each other or they might be into her. It's hard to tell. They're facing the girl, but they're staring at each other's erections while they jerk off. The men are very attractive: tall, well built and well groomed. They could be twins, actually—except for their cocks."

"Why's that?"

"Um …Okay, I get it—I think. I bet you have a whole stack of photos for me to scrutinize and label. You're after my perception of what's big, what's small, what's desirable and what's repulsive. You're collecting a bunch of subjective impressions, hoping to dispel the labels or erase the benchmarks that define attractiveness and ugliness. But you don't even know me. What qualifies me to be part of your

Subject X

representative sample?"

"I'm very impressed, Amy. You're quite sharp. However, you're far off the track in this case." Jeremy paused for a few seconds before continuing, "You're reading too much into what we're doing here. It's a simple survey about sex, sexual habits and sexual proclivities—that's all. We're not trying to change the world's standards. We simply want to help categorize them and better understand them. You'll answer our questions, sometimes with a simple 'yes' or 'no,' sometimes, if you would, with as much detail as you can provide."

"What's with the photograph?"

"We want to be assured that you're comfortable verbalizing your thoughts. Approximations aren't a lot of help to us. Anyway, I think we're good. Let's keep this moving."

"You mean because you heard me say 'cock.' So I passed the test?"

"We want you to be able to communicate your responses using precise language, yes. And no more photographs for you to detail. I promise." Jeremy searched through his notes, as if he'd lost his place.

"One of the men—the one with the Prince Albert piercing—has just finished ejaculating. Some of his come has landed on the woman's ass. Some of it's dripping down her thigh. I think I understand her expression better now. She wants to collect a dollop of jizz with her finger and have a taste. Yeah, I can tell she wants to spit that monster prick out of her mouth and suck the other guy's salty cream from her finger. What do *you* think?" Amy nodded at Brooke.

Brooke lowered her gaze to the computer tablet that was slipping across her tightly crossed legs like a wet bar of soap. "This isn't about me, Amy. Thank you for that interpretation, though. We're going to move on with the survey now."

Amy folded her hands together and let them fall to her

lap. She hadn't realized there would be a test she'd have to pass before advancing to Brooke and Jeremy's precious survey questions. She wanted the hundred bucks; but, geez, it was only a hundred bucks. She decided that one more outburst of pretentiousness from either of them and she was out of there. She had better things to do with her Friday than spell out a porn scene to a couple of tightly wound, pompous grad students. Screw the money. And screw Dylan. It was his fault she was in such a testy mood anyway.

***

"It's Cody's wedding, Amy. How am I not supposed to go?"

"I don't know, Dylan. Maybe you could explain to him that your girlfriend's a bitch and won't let you. You figure it out."

"He's one of my closest friends. I've known him since we were little kids. He was my fucking next-door neighbor, for god's sake. I'll be gone four days. I don't know why you're making such a big deal."

"Gee, Dylan, I don't know either. Four days at a resort in the Bahamas with all your buddies, and none of them are bringing their girlfriends. And I think it's kind of weird that we've been dating for a year, and you've never once mentioned your close friend Cody. If you need a break from me—from us—fine. Just say so."

"What's wrong, Amy? You've been acting, I don't know, different, the last few days. What did I do?"

"Why don't you tell me, Dylan? What did you do? Or should I ask *who* did you do?"

"You're crazy. If I wanted to screw around, I'd just leave you."

"Like this weekend? Is that why you stuffed boxes of condoms in your suitcase?"

"I don't need this shit, Amy. And I don't need to explain myself. Later."

"Have fun at the beach, Dylan. Hope the condoms hold out."

Amy lowered her eyes and listened as he escaped, waiting for the slam. What she heard was the ticking of a carry-on bag rolling across the tile floor and then the soft click of the apartment door as it latched shut. Dylan had left without snorting another word or making a scene.

"Yeah, have fun this weekend," Amy murmured to no one as she envisioned Dylan and his buds chilling on a powdery beach, hiding behind their impenetrable Ray-Bans. No doubt they'd be on the sand minutes after their plane touched down, surveying the sea of glistening skin and bite-sized bikinis.

That's when the idea hit her. An idea she would have never considered if her boyfriend hadn't thought of it first. She would have herself a fling—a one-nighter—a little entanglement without the attachment.

Amy stepped away from the notion for a moment to analyze her circumstances, her motivation—and her boyfriend—before slipping off her flip-flops and jumping headfirst into the murky water. She wasn't the impetuous type, and regrets always gnawed at her like a puppy on a new pair of Jimmy Choos.

It wasn't just Dylan's little Bahamian adventure that had set Amy off. It was really the sum total of shadowy hints, clues, signals and whispers that had brought her to this point. He'd been aloof lately, for starters. Amy had initially written this off as expected behavior for someone about to graduate from college. Although Dylan had sort of a game plan for life after school, he hadn't yet landed a job—or an interview. He had some life-defining moments ahead of him. As Amy saw it, that could make anyone a bit distant.

Amy still had a year of school left, which created yet

more issues for Dylan. As much as he had enjoyed his years at Ohio State, he was anxious to swap the cold Midwestern winters for anyplace that didn't budget for snow removal. So he was leaving soon, and they both knew it; they had just never talked about it.

Then there was the hang-up: Amy's, not Dylan's. He couldn't be blamed for this one. After a year of dating, it had yet to melt away, had yet to wither from her psyche as it should have. It was there when she rolled out of bed in the morning and watched him sleep, unclothed and unaffected. It was there when he sat across from her at the kitchen table, stirring a drizzle of honey through his bowl of oatmeal. And it was there every time she opened her Facebook page and scrutinized her profile picture: the one of both of them lazing on a blanket by the Olentangy River, two radiant smiles side by side. He was undeniably gorgeous, and she was certain that she was not.

Chapter Two

"Do you date, Amy?" Brooke bent forward as she asked the question. Her rose-colored wool blazer buckled at the lapels, exposing a clash of bright pink from her scooped-neck blouse.

Amy considered the motivation behind Brooke's awkward bob before she considered her question. A Ph.D. candidate in human sexual behavior—or any behavior, for that matter—did not twitch a muscle without understanding or considering the innuendo. Everything meant something to these people, from the nuance of a blinking eye to the glaring implication of an arched brow.

What was Brooke's intention? Amy had no idea. Maybe the cold, indifferent woman with stiff, ash-brown hair brushed with an apparent iron fist wanted her to notice her breasts, wanted her to know there was another female in the room.

Amy contemplated what Brooke had nudged her to contemplate: what lurked beneath the dense woolen fibers, blocky shoulder pads and gaudy brass buttons of her blazer. The woman's tits weren't small, most likely; but Amy needed more clues, more particulars. Maybe there was some significance to Brooke's black, thick-rimmed glasses beyond a deluded proclamation of intelligence. She wasn't a hipster, but she was definitely trying to declare herself as something.

"Yes. I date. Are you sure that's a good question? I mean, what constitutes a date anymore? Do I go out with guys? Yes."

"How long have you been dating?" Jeremy asked quickly, heading off a potential duel and a certain waste of time. He'd been evaluating the temperature and wanted to lower the thermostat before the room became uncomfortably warm.

"About five years."

"You started dating when you were fifteen then?"

"I think so."

"These can be considered open-ended questions." Brooke glared at Amy, itching for something juicier than a "yes" or "no," something that might catalog the girl as a prude or perhaps a slut.

"Then maybe you should consider asking them as open-ended questions." Amy scanned the room, trying to remember where she had put her purse, assuming she was about to be dismissed, wondering if she'd receive any portion of the hundred dollars she'd been promised.

"Approximately how many men would you say you have dated?" Jeremy asked, hoping to keep Amy in her chair.

"Lots." Amy was surprised to be asked another question, but hardly surprised by the inanity of it.

Amy's attention was suddenly diverted by the sound of a bird scraping against one of the improbably tall windows lining the eastern stretch of the room. She became lost in the crystal-clear sheets of glass and the neatly manicured knots of hydrangeas just beyond.

"Are you a virgin?" Jeremy posed the question. Brooke squinted over her glasses, stealing a glimpse of the girl.

Past the orderly slip of garden stood more of the same building. It was an oddly positioned annex that ran alongside the original structure. Although it had been added some years later, the rambling brick wing mirrored the vintage architectural style of the original. The windows of the two buildings lined up perfectly; and without any coverings, it was easy to spy into someone else's life just on the other side of the bushes across the narrow courtyard.

"I was."

"What exactly do you mean?" Brooke asked, a flush of frustration pecking at her cheeks, adding another awkward hue to her already skirmishing rose-colored blazer and bright pink blouse.

"What do you think I mean?"

"I think you are no longer a virgin, but that's all I can deduce from your reply. Maybe we haven't been clear enough regarding our expectations here, Amy. We'd appreciate it if you would elaborate more; take our questions and run with them, if you will. We would have just handed you a questionnaire and a pencil if we were seeking terse, fill-in-the-blank answers."

There wasn't anyone in the room across the courtyard, yet it still offered a soothing diversion for someone desperate to escape from a long, uncomfortable afternoon of asinine questioning. There were things to consider, like what the room was used for and why it was currently unoccupied.

"I get it. Really, I do. You want me to ramble when I can. I've slept with—sorry, fucked—about, I don't know, half a dozen guys. Some of those guys I screwed lots of times—a couple of them, maybe twice. I don't have sex just to have sex. I have to have real feelings for someone. I guess that's love, right? I don't know—maybe not. I have to at least feel …something special about a guy before I want to fuck him."

"Are you currently in love?" Jeremy asked.

"I'm not sure. I just told you that I have difficulty defining love. I'm currently in a relationship, if that's what you're asking. At least I think I am."

***

She couldn't keep her eyes closed, not that she wanted to. It was only their second time; and, like the first, it was spontaneous, instinctual. She wanted a better look at him, eager to understand the emotion behind his enthusiasm, his appetite. She wanted to peer into his clear brown eyes when she came. She wanted to consume all of him.

The steady cascade of thoughtful gifts he'd given her since their first date wasn't what had prompted her to fold this time. She loved the small, hand-painted pots filled with pansies, marigolds and African violets. And she had a weakness for the fresh-baked cookies and mixed berry pie he'd purchased from a local farmers' market. He could have given her unsurprising bunches of flowers, boxes of chocolates or nothing at all and she would have been happy.

No, there was something else about him, some other reason her ankles were wrapped behind his thighs, urging him deeper. He was a romantic, for sure, a quality she was unfamiliar with in a boyfriend. He was handsome too, gifted with enough good looks to turn the heads of women trapped in neck braces; she'd seen it happen—twice. He was fun and he was funny. He was smart and he was clever. And he seemed to truly care for her. He was a mystery she hoped to unravel, to understand. And now, embracing his warmth as he pressed into her, she wanted to look at him and find a reason to settle her unease.

"You're the prettiest girl in the whole world, Amy."

No, don't say another word, Dylan, she whispered to herself. *Don't change how I feel right now, the scent of you nuzzling my heart, distorting my common sense.*

Dylan ran his fingers through Amy's long, toffee-colored hair, massaging her scalp, playing with her thoughts. His elbows supported only some of his weight as he imposed, time and again, on her comforting, responsive body. His chest skated over her breasts, harassing her stiff, responsive nipples, egging them on, provoking her passion.

Amy caressed all accessible parts of him from the middle of his back down to his firm round ass, sensing, feeling his pounding heart and his pressing need for her— and for his release. Her fingers dug into the flesh of his cheeks, pulling him close and then closer until he was nestled against her clit, crowding it, embracing it, inciting it to take her where she wanted to go. Spasms of pleasure echoed through her, a charge of energy that rapidly dissolved to mellow impotence and a soothed, unknotted feeling.

"That was nice, Amy—very nice."

"Shit, Dylan. That was beyond nice. You threw me some kind of knockout punch. I hope you weren't thinking we'd be going anywhere tonight. I can't move."

"Perfect. I'll stay here with you, if that's okay."

"Yeah. I would like that."

The wrinkled white sheet clawed at their hips and legs, leaving the rest of them exposed. They gazed at each other, thinking about what they had just done—and wondering when they'd do it again.

***

"Would you consider yourself a flirt, Amy?" Jeremy uncrossed then re-crossed his legs as he asked.

"Isn't everyone a flirt? Am I a cock tease? Is that what you meant to ask?"

Jeremy didn't flinch. He didn't respond either. Amy was a smart girl, but her patronizing retorts had become trying. He just wanted to muscle through this study and be done with it. She was the first of many—one girl out of twenty—that he was scheduled to interview. He didn't think he'd make it, not if all the respondents were like her.

He was also bothered by Brooke's behavior. She didn't seem to be on the same page as he. This was a small sample study, and it was important for him and Brooke to stay out of the way. He didn't want the respondents to be given the opportunity to contemplate or feed on his or Brooke's emotions.

Brooke was already too tight, too visible. He wished he'd gotten to know her better before they'd decided to team up. If he had spent some time with her off the academic stage, having a real-world conversation while sharing a bottle of wine perhaps, he might understand her better now.

"You're not going to answer me—okay." Amy rolled her eyes in a feeble attempt to express her annoyance before continuing, "Am I a flirt? Hmm. Yes, I'm a flirt. That's why I wear makeup, I suppose. That's why I shop for clothes that fit me well, highlight my assets and mask my flaws. Could be, subconsciously, I guess, the reason I'm sitting the way I am now."

Amy knew they'd both look. Even though she'd been sitting across from them all this time, they'd still glance at her legs. After all, she'd just invited them to do so. Brooke would search for the flaws she had alluded to. Jeremy would frisk her with his eyes, hunting for previously unnoticed assets. They did not disappoint.

As she watched them take the bait, Amy wondered if they had found what they were looking for. She wanted to jump into Jeremy's head, read his thoughts, get his appraisal. After all, if she were going to pursue hot, messy revenge sex this weekend, she wouldn't mind an independent assessment. Yeah, she'd better be a flirt, she thought. Otherwise it could be a frustrating, lonely weekend.

Jeremy tilted his iPad that had been lying smoothly across his lap, until it was angled toward his face. He stared at it as if it had become broken or perhaps illegible. He wanted to push on with the survey, but he needed to digest some things first, keep his head steady.

He had provoked the girl, and so had Brooke. They had asked her to elaborate, to be candid and expansive with her answers. Now she was provoking them. He had caught Brooke contemplating Amy's posture, attitude and legs. And Amy had caught him doing the same. It was a natural response—unavoidable really—especially with someone who had suddenly, unexpectedly, become so …seductive.

It wasn't just the lengthy ribbons of sun-kissed hair, spilling without rhythm over her fluid shoulders and across her brow, nor was it her unclouded, probing brown eyes or slender, toned body. It wasn't even her persistent saucy insolence that had disturbed his balance and threatened his poise. It was the way all those things collaborated, the way they harmonized.

That skirt of Amy's, so short, so revealing; even with her knees pressed together, he could see more of her than he had hoped to see. In another setting, under different circumstances, he would revel in the hypnotic sweep of skin between her knee-high black leather boots and the hem of her gray tweed miniskirt. And he would gladly scrutinize the compact, crescent curves parading beneath her clingy, striped sweater.

But he would have to shut his eyes to these distractions today. This study was important to him and to Brooke. He needed to expose Amy's thoughts, not her thighs. It wouldn't be easy. She was disclosing her sexual proclivities to him, for god's sake.

Chapter Three

Brooke sensed she should take the reins for a while to give Jeremy a needed break. As a doctoral candidate in human sexual behavior, she was skilled at detecting subtle tics of disquietude, especially when rooted in sexual friction. But she didn't need a degree to know Jeremy was drifting, thrown off course by a young woman brandishing her instinctive wiles.

"Amy, we're at a bit of a fork in the road here, and I'm going to give you the option of which direction we should take. I have a series of questions about kissing and cuddling, for instance. As an example, I might provide you a list of different kinds of kisses, everything from a peck on the cheek say, to a dance with your partner's tongue, and then ask you to tell me what that kiss means to you. Is it romantic? Could it be romantic? Could it be sexually stimulating? Is it always sexually stimulating? You get the picture. Or we could take this down another path, one that would be more ...personally intrusive. You've demonstrated a willingness to be candid with us. We would need you to continue to say what you feel and why you feel, if you choose this path. We would also need you to commit to spending an extra hour or so with us this afternoon. For that, you'll be compensated with an additional hundred dollars. Keep in mind your name will never be associated with our study results. You'll always be referred to as 'Subject X,' for instance. Jeremy and I are the only ones who will be aware of your identity. I'll leave it to you."

"Okay—I think. I'll give option two a try. So, at the end of the session, I'll get a check for two hundred dollars?"

"Cash."

Even better, Amy thought. If this were going to get nasty,

and if Brooke and Jeremy were going to crowd her head with their little sexual interrogation, or, more precisely, if she were going to fill their heads with whatever warped responses they begged for, then she would certainly be primed for her man-hunting expedition later. And with two hundred cash in her purse, she could score herself a hell of a one-night stand *and* a nice pair of new shoes.

"Go ahead, ask away."

"Alright. Are you comfortable with your body, Amy?"

"It's my body. I try to take good care of it. I eat a pretty healthy diet and usually get to the Student Rec Center a few times a week, you know, take a couple of yoga classes, get in a couple of workouts. When I have the time, I'll go for a jog around campus. That's about all a girl can do, right?"

"Please answer the question, Amy. Are you comfortable with your body?"

Amy scrutinized the pair of grad students sitting across from her, trying to read their poker-faced stares, itching for their nearly professional opinions of her potential as a seductress.

"No, I'm not." Amy didn't have to ask Brooke if she wanted details. Of course she did. This was what they were paying her the extra hundred bucks for and why they had promised her the designation 'Subject X.' "Okay, here goes," she continued. "It was the end of fall semester my sophomore year. I had joined a sorority, just like every other sophomore girl searching for a niche, a new identity and, I guess, an easy way to meet boys. The sisters were mostly pretty nice and, aside from the few stereotypical stuck-up sorority bitches, very helpful—you know, glad to give advice on everything from picking the right classes to picking the right bars. So, as I'm sure you know, you can't just sign up to be a member of a sorority. To begin with, there's this whole antiquated, somewhat discriminatory, very unreasonable vetting process just to become a pledge. It's worse than applying for an unlimited line of credit, right, Brooke? You pledged a sorority, I bet."

"Go on."

"Okay, so it was my last week as a pledge—hell week. Just a few more days and I'd be an active—a permanent, card-carrying member. I was so spellbound, so caught up in the sisterhood crap that I would do pretty much anything the actives asked of me. By this time there wasn't one girl in my pledge class who wouldn't have peed in the middle of High Street just to become a full-fledged sister. Anyway, Friday morning of hell week, a group of actives cornered me and my closest pledge friend, Leah, as we were leaving the house on our way to class. Leah was this sweet, bright girl with giant tits and platinum blonde hair. She might as well have had a target on her ass too, the way all the actives treated her. So they blindfolded us with these awful pig masks that had pieces of tape over the eyeholes, stripped us bare and then wrapped bath towels around us. We were informed that we'd be taking a little stroll down the block. They guided us by grabbing onto our elbows and dragging us along, chirping out warnings just before we'd stumble over curbs or pieces of broken sidewalk. They'd scream 'Step up!' or 'Step down!' at the top of their lungs like every twenty seconds. The screaming was almost as embarrassing as being seen walking around in a towel. They led us around like this for a while until we reached a building. For all I could tell, we had circled back around to our house. At least that's what I had hoped. I knew right away, though, that we were someplace else. It didn't smell at all like our sorority."

"Amy"—Brooke stole a glance at her watch as she grumbled out the girl's name—"I'm not sure we need all this back story. We're looking for detail, but only if it has direct relevance to our question."

"I thought it might; but, whatever. I'm happy to cut to the chase. Anyway, Brooke, it turns out they had dragged Leah and me to the community shower room of a popular fraternity, one our sorority socialized with fairly regularly. We still didn't know where we were. It was quiet except for some faint whispering sounds. We were commanded to sing our sorority rush song—loud—and then sing it again louder. As we sang it the second time, one of the actives jerked the towels from our bodies. The abrupt sensation of total nudity jolted us, and we stopped singing momentarily. Then the actives screamed at us to start over. All of a sudden water began to pour from the dozen or so showerheads in the room. Leah and I were naked, soaked, and still couldn't see a damn thing. When I heard the laughter, that's when I pulled off my mask. Leah pulled hers off too. Crowded in the entryway to the shower room were as many fucking fraternity boys' faces as would fit. They were all laughing—laughing and pointing. We tried to cover ourselves as best we could with our hands, but you know how well that works. That's when I heard it, not just from one of the boys but from a bunch of them:

"Nice tits, Blondie!"

"Hey, Steve's tits are bigger than the other chick's!"

"Are you kidding? All our tits are bigger than hers!"

"Seriously they were acting like a bunch of sixth graders which, I guess, makes sense since that's when their maturity must have peaked and locked into place. We had no choice but to force our way out of the shower and pray our future sorority sisters would be waiting for us with some clothes. When we got to the showers' doorway, the crowd of boys stepped aside, as if they were afraid of being arrested for harassing and touching unenthused, naked girls. We scanned the hallway for the actives but couldn't find them. They had already left. That's when I met him."

"Met who?" Brooke asked.

"Dylan. My boyfriend. Here was this cute guy leaning against the hallway wall, one hand punched halfway into a pocket of his fatigued jeans, the other clenching two folded

M.L. Joslyn

bath towels. He offered them to us, insisted actually, and then apologized for his fraternity brothers' behavior, referring to them as "mostly idiots." He kept his head turned from us as he spoke. At the time I wasn't sure if he were hoping to avoid a potentially pitiful display of female nudity or if he were behaving like a gentleman. He had heard the girls from our house squealing as they ran from the scene and claimed it wasn't too difficult to piece together what had happened. He said it was a regular occurrence this time of year. Anyway, it wasn't like I was totally traumatized by the experience; but it's one of those things I've never been able to shake, you know? It's always kind of there, waiting for me to remember. Until recently I hadn't given up on my breasts. I kept thinking I just needed to stay patient, and maybe one day I'd wake up with C cups and never have to brood about them again. So that's my explanation as to why I'm not totally comfortable with my body. Honestly, though, I wouldn't have this fucked-up insecurity if it weren't for that drama of more than three years ago."

"Thank you for your candor, Amy." Brooke stopped typing on her tablet and looked at the girl across the way. She'd gotten what she had asked for: a defense of a response and a possible foundation for her future responses. She didn't feel bad for Amy, and she wasn't about to offer any tonic to repair her issues. This was a study, and her job was to collect information and formulate a hypothesis based on that information. Besides, she didn't really believe her. Amy was pretty—sexy, even. She couldn't imagine her having any trouble attracting a man—or a woman, if that were her bent. The second the girl had entered the room, Brooke had noticed, had started judging, comparing. Where Amy was willowy, Brooke was curvy. Where Amy was seductive, Brooke was uninviting. And where Amy was strong and insolent, Brooke was strong …and insolent.

Jeremy had a different take on Amy's story. He wasn't

20

comparing her to anyone. He was trying to understand her lingering insecurities, wondering why she had let them fester so long. He wished he could have a couple hours alone with her to help erase the senseless anxiety precipitated by a purposeless, inconsequential event. The incident was nothing more than an inane sorority prank designed to humiliate.

In Jeremy's mind he couldn't imagine anyone making light of Amy's appearance, not unless they were envious of her or understood they had no chance with her, sexually speaking. She wasn't just a pretty girl. She was smart, perceptive and sharp-witted. And to Jeremy her tits were perfect: perfectly shaped, perfectly sized and perfectly tempting. They influenced the fit of her sweater, giving it more allure than it deserved. Her clothes hadn't been chosen to enhance the appeal of her figure; her figure enhanced the appeal of her clothes. But these things couldn't matter to Jeremy—not now. He had to move on and learn more about her, her sexual history and her sexual ...inclinations.

"Amy, how old were you when you first had sexual intercourse?"

"Eighteen. It was after my high school graduation party. Wait—it was actually *during* my high school graduation party. The school or planning committee or whoever was responsible for organizing this thing had rented the clubhouse at a really nice country club. You know, the sort of place that's so fancy it's beyond pretentious, like the carpet is so thick you get a workout just walking around in heels?

"I had gone out with this guy, Kyle, only a handful of times; but I had known him for years, being classmates and everything. We went to the party with his best friend and his best friend's girlfriend. Both Kyle and his buddy had flasks of vodka stashed in their pants, so after about a half-hour at this thing, we were all pretty tipsy, having a lot of fun, rolling about this huge, overstuffed leather couch.

M.L. Joslyn

"It didn't take long before the other couple was all over each other, pawing, kissing, and whispering love notes, I guess, back and forth. Pretty soon they disappeared, stumbling off somewhere away from all the activity. "I remember the look on Kyle's face then. He had this odd, crooked sort of smile; and his eyes gave me the once-over, I don't know, like he'd just had the first good idea of his life. That's when he kissed me. He just leaned in and went for it. I have to admit I was attracted to the guy. He'd been some sort of track star at our school, and all the girls thought he was pretty hot. His ass had been unofficially ranked the tightest and sexiest of all the boys in our class. I guess I agreed. I wasn't opposed to him kissing me, obviously.

"When he reached for my hand, he nodded toward his friends, or at least in the direction of where they'd headed. I knew what he wanted. I wanted it too. I was curious more than anything. I know this sounds horrible, but I just wanted to get it over with. We found a dimly lit room filled with round banquet tables but otherwise empty. Kyle threw a few tablecloths on the floor, and that was that. It didn't last long. It was a mess really, just a fascinating, awful mess."

That should satisfy them, Amy thought. Not too much back story, just enough detail. She considered giving them more and would have, if Brooke weren't such a fussy bitch.

***

"I can take off my own clothes, Kyle. Don't rip my dress–seriously. I didn't bring a spare."

"C'mon, Amy. Let me look at you, babe."

"Do you have a condom?"

"Right here."

"Alright. It goes on now. Let me put it on you."

"I've got to take my pants off first, Amy. Give me a second."

22

Amy wasn't sure what to expect. She'd seen a few penises before, most of them in the sex education textbook she'd been forced to read her freshman year, and then a couple more when her parents had inadvertently taken her to a clothing-optional beach in the Caribbean a year later. She was forced to study the textbook for a whole school year; she was at the beach for about two minutes. What she had yet to see, at least up close and in person, was an erect penis. She wanted to see her first one—and touch her first one—but she wasn't sure the first would be the one she'd want inside her.

While Kyle fumbled with his pants, Amy slipped out of her dress and unhooked her bra, exposing herself, almost, to the boy with the substantial stiffy in his shorts. She couldn't take her eyes off it. She was mesmerized by the way it pressed with insistence against the overtaxed fabric.

Kyle's eyes darted between Amy's breasts and the small triangle of fabric that covered her feverish pussy; he lowered his shorts to the floor and quickly pushed them out of the way. Amy couldn't help herself; she reached for his huge cock with both of her hands, anxious to feel its pulsing power, eager to squeeze it and gauge its resiliency. It was enormous, at least to her. She wasn't sure if her pussy could ingest such a monster. And she couldn't comprehend how something so large, so imposing, might be pleasurable in the slightest.

It wasn't as if she had never masturbated, had never slid a vibrator over her folds and let it sneak through her hatch as if by accident—as if she weren't paying attention. But Kyle's cock was much bigger than her vibe, and it was attached to something, someone, whom she did not control.

Amy tore the wrapper from the flesh-shaded condom and, with hands weakened by the prevailing uncertainties, clutched the lubricated circle of latex, knowing what to do, but afraid to do it. A dozen "what-ifs" wheeled through her vodka-stained mind as she unrolled the sheath down his shaft, scrutinizing every inch and every ridge. Her hand warmed from the heat of his thumping, swollen cock. She wanted to leave it there, wrapped around this curiosity, this unfamiliar, fascinating amusement. But Kyle was insistent, and soon she was on her back, panties tossed to the floor, legs spread.

"I don't think that's the hole you're looking for, Kyle. Here, let me help." Amy reached for the tip of his cock, her fingers grazing the springy reservoir end of the condom. She wished she could watch it fill with his come. She wanted to fuck him, see what it was all about, get the first one out of the way. But what she was really hungry for was another look—a closer inspection—an inch-by-inch exploration of the instrument he was still learning to play. It was too late for that, though—maybe. She closed her eyes and guided him through her wet slit.

"Okay—enough." Amy pressed her palms against Kyle's shoulders, leveraging him from her chest. Two strokes, maybe three—that's all she'd given him. She wished it had felt better, been more comfortable; but she couldn't endure any more of his probing, thick pole. It was obviously going to take more than three strokes for those oft-rumored swells of snowballing pleasure to kick in, and she didn't have the willpower or desire to discover exactly how many it would take. She wished penises came in starter sizes, or were adjustable, like those pick-your-comfort-level air mattresses.

"But ..."

"I know, I know. Don't worry. I'll take care of you. Up on your knees—c'mon."

"I guess."

There it was, inches from her face, throbbing to the beat of his heart. It appeared ready to explode. She rushed to remove the condom so she could see, feel—and if the planets were perfectly aligned—taste what all the fuss, good and bad, was about.

"This comes off now—before you do." Amy curled her hand around the base of Kyle's prick and pushed the condom up and away, as if she were dislodging a rubber band from a rolled-up newspaper. "When you come, come on me, okay?"

Kyle's eyes did all the answering. They were already latched on to Amy's body, searching for the most compelling target. Amy sensed his uncertainty and decided to make things easier for him. She looked him in the eyes, cupped her tits in her hands and began to squeeze. Kyle seemed even more confused.

"Am I supposed to, you know, do you want me to, uh, I guess I'm supposed to jerk off?" Kyle asked, scanning the room like a nervous squirrel.

"Oh shit, sorry." It wasn't that Amy expected his cock to explode on its own. She was hoping to watch as he masturbated to orgasm. The anticipation of him stroking himself had her hotter, wetter than she had been before he'd plunged his huge dick inside her. "Why don't you show me how you like it?"

"What?"

"Show me how you want me to stroke it."

"That's kind of … you mean you want me to teach you how to jerk me off?"

"Yeah. Some guys like a soft touch and some guys like to really squeeze it, right? Show me and I'll do it."

"Okay. Like this, I guess."

Amy inched closer to Kyle's cock, hypnotized by the taut, yet fluid covering of skin that staggered beneath his loose grip. His hard prick lurched back and forth through a tunnel of curled fingers formed by a practiced hand, escaping, retreating, escaping, retreating. He was fucking, not her, but his hand. Amy's head filled with a mess of tangled thoughts. Watching him masturbate was the biggest turn-on of her evening, and she was certain that wasn't right, wasn't normal. She wanted to come, could sense her orgasm lying

M.L. Joslyn

low, waiting for the proper moment. She didn't want him inside her, not now, not after the pain.

She wished he would reach for her pussy with his free hand and massage her clit. But she knew he wouldn't get it right, wouldn't be able to navigate through the thick pads of sheltering flesh that held it captive; and now wasn't the time for a lesson. She could get herself off later if she needed to or still wanted to. All she really wanted was to watch him come—with his own hand.

"That is so sexy, Kyle. You're really turning me on. Come on my tits, okay?"

"I don't have much choice, Amy. Oh god, squeeze those babies for me. Squeeze them!"

Kyle stopped fucking his hand, but his fingers remained rooted to his cock. With a firm grip he began to tug, once, twice and then again, as if he were teaching the monster a lesson or dispensing punishment for something it had done, or was about to do. He pulled hard once more, the skin of his prick stretched to its limit. The tiny slit at the tip, which until now had seemed an innocent mistake of nature, a minor nick in an otherwise flawless crown, gaped open. A hesitant second later, a weak dash of come leapt from it, followed by a much stronger, much thicker rush. The milky cream pulsed in measured waves, until there was no more. Kyle's eyes closed. He was no longer leering at his target, no longer needing it to hasten his release.

Amy ran a finger through the warm liquid pooling across her belly and brought it to her face. She inhaled cautiously at first, hoping she'd be fond of the aroma, but fearful of finding it repellent. A heady charge of pine, wild cherries and something clean or fresh, she wasn't certain, hit her senses, making her even hotter, hornier. She popped her juiced-up finger in her mouth and sucked hard. She liked it. She loved it. She wanted more. Two fingers' worth this time, quickly, while he wasn't looking, while he was still lost in the aftermath.

Amy continued to wipe her belly clean, drinking from her fingers, savoring the salty, sweet essence of ...some man. The man was lying next to her, lost in a dream of his own, his cock still thick, but relaxed, spent.

With two fingers in her mouth and four on her mound, it didn't take her long. She knew what Kyle didn't know—would never know—and she hurriedly smothered her arousal, whimpering as she came.

"Amy, can I, do you mind if I ask you something?" Kyle, awakened by the faint, provocative sounds, rolled onto his side, facing Amy. With a thick fist, he braced his head.

"Sure."

"Did you come when I, when we ...?"

"When you were inside me. Yeah."

"Oh, okay. That was pretty nice. I'm sorry if I ..."

"Shhh. Nothing to be sorry about. It was pretty nice for me too. I'm not sure I want to go back to the party."

"I was hoping you'd say that."

"You're a cool guy, Kyle."

Chapter Four

A light flickered in the room across the courtyard, pulling Amy from her daydream and from the tediously trying pair of Ph.D. candidates sitting on the other side of the low-slung table. Maybe it hadn't been just a flicker, she considered with dismay. Had she been so lost in her thoughts that she'd missed someone in the room, someone who'd been using it for its intended purpose? Maybe they'd been peering in her direction and were wondering about her, the intriguing girl in the chair. If she could see into their room, they could see into hers. Not fair, she thought. *Come back. Show me who you are, and what you were doing in there.*

Amy turned her focus back to Brooke and Jeremy. They were both typing on their iPads. Were they sending notes back and forth to each other? Had she said something to provoke them? Maybe, Amy thought, she'd given them too much personal information, or maybe they were concerned that she was still withholding the good stuff. Or, most likely, she'd just bored them into playing some sort of computer game.

"Give us a second, Amy." Brooke spoke as if she were stressing over her Ms. Pac-Man's ability to devour the scurrying, blinking ghosts before they could make it back to the safety of their pen.

"Take your time." Amy reached for her purse and began pawing through the clutter of keys, highlighters, lipsticks, and wrinkled singles, hoping to run into a piece of gum. Pushing aside her Hello Kitty address book, the one filled with precisely zero addresses but close to twenty kitten face doodles, she noticed her cell phone's flashing, green alert light silently beckoning.

Despite Brooke and Jeremy's possibly misguided

judgments, Amy considered herself well mannered, and had silenced her phone as soon as she had stepped into the building. But since her interviewers were taking some kind of break, she didn't consider it discourteous to check her messages.

There was just one, and it was a text from Dylan: *"I miss you. I'll call soon."* After a two-second bout of ill-considered elation, Amy fell back to earth; and with the speed of a cheetah chasing down a gazelle, she typed a reply: *"Don't call—in an interview."*

She grabbed her purse and sent her phone back into the abyss. *That should give him something to think about.* Dylan hadn't known about her signing up for a study, and this was the sort of message that would distress him, at least a little. He always wanted to know what she was up to – as if he were concerned.

"Do men give you more comfort than women? Sexually speaking, that is." Brooke uncrossed her legs, angled them away from Amy and then tugged at the hem of her skirt.

"It's always about sex, isn't it?" Amy waited for a response but should have known better. "Men do, I suppose."

"You suppose?"

"I suppose."

Damn it, girl, Brooke declared silently. You know the rules. Why can't you give me what I'm looking for? "I'll need more than 'I suppose'."

"Okay. I suppose men comfort me, sexually speaking, that is, more than women."

Brooke understood that Amy considered her response complete, was defending her privacy and had said all she was going to say. She hadn't stated unequivocally that men, only men, gave her comfort. She'd left the door open, at least a little. Not that Brooke was personally interested. Her job was to collect information from twenty respondents, evaluate the data and form a report. Human sexual behavior was her field or would soon be her field, professionally speaking. She found it irritating that everyone—her professors, her students and even her study subjects—seemed to forget, or at least ignore, that she was human too. She was always in control, of course. She had never, nor would she ever, behave inappropriately.

But still, Brooke was a sexual being with the same wants, needs and desires as any other sexual being. She tried to hide it behind indelicate, boring glasses and frumpish clothing. She even tried to camouflage her humanness with an expressionless façade and a flat, uninflected voice. It was all a pretense. Maybe someday, when she was an established therapist, she could allow herself to be more approachable, more vulnerable. But it was too soon for that … and too risky.

As for now, she'd sometimes allow her mind to drift, just a little, to contemplate the things anyone with a healthy sex drive might contemplate. For instance, she'd been assessing the man in the chair next to her all day, wondering how gentle or forceful he'd be in bed. But it was only in the last few minutes that she'd stopped assessing and started …imagining. Those piercing, pale blue eyes of his—what would they do to her when she was inches from them, when he was fucking her, when they were sharing breaths? Would she melt into his arms? Probably. Would she want to take every inch of him? Definitely. And, what *about* those inches? What did they look like when he was all worked up and ready to put them to use? How would they taste when they danced with her tongue? And how would they fill her and bring her pleasure? She wanted answers, but she couldn't have them. She would never allow herself to ask the questions.

"Alright, Amy. Let's move on then."

"Go ahead, ask."

It was the girl. She was the reason Brooke had suddenly

surrendered to her hard-wired desires and the reason she was uncomfortably, inappropriately wet. Maybe Amy wasn't the prettiest or most sensual girl she had ever counseled, examined or interviewed; but there was something innocent and …naughty about her.

Perhaps it was her soft voice, the way it remained unobtrusive while it petitioned for attention. As Amy spit vulgarities against Brooke's crumbling façade, they agitated *and* aroused, each a caressing, taunting catalyst. Or perhaps it was the girl's lack of self-confidence—it gave her an aura of vulnerability and made her seem more available, obtainable.

Brooke was supposed to be able to identify cause and effect. If given time to analyze the scene, she could have easily determined the psychosocial reason for her response to the girl. But again she was human, and for now her overriding instincts were in the way.

"Have you ever had sex with a woman?" Brooke asked. She glanced at Jeremy and caught him scanning his notes, searching for the question. He wouldn't find it.

"Okay, well, I can't say that I have."

"You seem uncertain."

"To be honest, it's something I have considered. I've never told anyone this, but I've been attracted, sexually, to girls before. It's not anything I've ever acted on but, yeah, I've thought about it and that's as far as it went."

"Were any of these girls you've been …tempted by, let's say, lesbians or bisexuals?"

"It's odd that you ask, but yeah. I guess when I know they're open to a sexual relationship with another woman, that's when I consider the possibilities."

"Why do you think you've never acted on your interest?" Brooke leaned forward, hoping to induce a response.

"I think I just want to kiss and stop there. That's why, I guess. I don't know, maybe I would want to take it further if I ever got that far. I doubt I'll ever know."

"Why's that?"

"I love men. They satisfy me, make me happy. Girls are ...comfortable, I suppose I'd say. They're less challenging, sometimes more understanding, I guess."

"Understanding of what?"

"Of other women. Men have all these expectations, all these notions of what a woman should be, right? You can't help but wonder if you're woman enough for them. Am I feminine enough? Am I pretty enough? Can I give him everything another woman could? I think, and I may be wrong, but women are more forgiving when it comes to sex. We might appreciate another woman's body for what it is, rather than what it could be, or should be. Having said that, I love the feeling of a man on top of me or under me. I don't think anything could satisfy me like a man's cock. So, that's it, I suppose. I find the idea of sex with another woman intriguing, but again, I love men."

Jeremy found the back-and-forth between Brooke and Amy not only educational but also entertaining. He listened carefully, of course, fascinated by the seesawing cadence, pitch and inflection of their voices. Brooke had not only veered off the map with her questioning, she'd also broken from her colorless, vapid persona, as if she were suddenly vested in the study, as if it were actually meaningful to her. And Amy had turned a corner of sorts as well. She was less protective of her feelings, had dropped the shield at least a little. She had become more candid and more vulnerable.

But Jeremy hadn't just been listening. He'd been watching, observing ...contemplating. Brooke and Amy's volleys of non-verbal cues, articulated but unvoiced implications, had been intense and more telling than their spoken words. The way their eyes connected, then disconnected from each other: veered right, then left, up, then down. Their posture, the way they held their hands, the positioning of their legs, every movement expressive and revealing.

He hadn't considered Brooke in this light before. She was an academic, the sort of intellectual Jeremy had befriended, studied with and worked with often. He knew her just as he'd known all the others. He could effortlessly project her future, write her biography and carve her epitaph. Brooke would dedicate herself to her career, to her research and possibly, if the stars aligned, to another academic, someone with a like mind. Her interests were narrow, her desire for diversions limited.

But this was a new Brooke emerging: a surprise wrapped in an old woman's blazer and nerd glasses. He would have never guessed.

"May I jump in?" Jeremy wasn't ready to leave the subject—not yet. "Just one more question before we move along. You've stated your preference for men sexually, but you mentioned that you have considered sleeping with a woman. When you've had these thoughts, Amy, do you picture yourself in the assertive position or the subordinate position?"

What a self-serving, impolite bend of the rules. Shame on you, Jeremy murmured to the demon on his shoulder. *But go ahead, Amy. Tell me about you and your girlfriend. What sort of kiss did you have in mind for her? Hmm? Would you want to fuck her, or would you want her to strap one on and take you from behind so you couldn't see her, only picture her. Where would your lips be? Where would you want hers to be? On your pussy, I bet. Or maybe somewhere else, yeah, like sucking on those perfect little peaches of yours. You don't want someone like Brooke, I can tell. She may want you—god knows she wants someone—but you don't want the likes of her. You want someone as lithe as you. Maybe a flower child, right? A girl with long, straight hair choked back by a hand-woven head wrap dotted with tiny crystals. She has a few curls above her split too, doesn't she? She keeps them trim, just for you, just in case you visit. And she smells great, I bet, huh? Like jasmine or patchouli or maybe like springtime when it's early in the morning and the light breezes carry the songs of young birds that are learning, hoping to fly.*

"I don't picture myself in either the traditional male role or the traditional female role, if that's what you're asking. I only imagine myself experimenting, you know, playing around, touching, tasting. It wouldn't be a turn-on for me if my partner weren't my—I'm not sure how to best define it—equal."

Yeah, someone just like you, Amy. You're done with each other now, aren't you? I can tell. I can see it in the way you're holding each other, stroking each other with just the tips of your fingers, those careful, manicured nails etching faded love notes across the other's creamy skin. Are you ready for me? Both of you? You can have me now. Here's my cock, Amy. Don't ever doubt if you're pretty enough or feminine enough. I swear I've never been harder. Share it with your friend and then share your friend with me. I'll let you hold me, toy with me, take me where you want me to go. Use your hands, your mouths, your pussies, whatever you like. And then it will be my turn. I want you to lie together, heat touching heat, so I can have you both at the same time. My tongue will slide from one of you to the other, if you don't mind. You're so delicious and I'm so ravenous. I can taste you already. I want to breathe you in, and then I want to make you come. I want to hear how you sound when you have your orgasm. And then I'll leave. It's okay. Get some rest. Hold each other. I can return tomorrow.

"Thank you, Amy." Jeremy cloaked his sentiments beneath a composed tongue. "We're anxious to gather more of your thoughts, so it's best we move on."

Chapter Five

An arc of heavy clouds skated across the sky, plugging the last persistent holes of daylight. The sudden shift to darkness caught Amy's attention, drawing her gaze from the increasingly cryptic pair seated across from her to the tall windows lining the eastern wall of the room.

It was only mid-afternoon, but nature had declared it time for the sun to go away, maybe for a little while, maybe for the day. Amy could still see past the slim break of nurtured plants and tended mounds of loam into the empty room across the courtyard. Or maybe it wasn't empty. There was movement, something or someone floating from right to left in the furthest reach of the space. What was it? Who was it?

"Amy, what method of birth control do you prefer to use?"

Brooke's question lingered in the air, waiting for Amy to grab and do something with, but she didn't want to. Not because it belonged on a form questionnaire or that it seemed irrelevant to the recent run of interrogation, but because it had pulled her back into the room, away from the curious situation across the garden.

"I'm on the pill. I use the pill. What do I prefer? I prefer condoms."

"Why would you use the pill if you prefer condoms?"

The someone or something had turned on a singular lamp, dispatching a yellowish-white glow through the room. Shadows pooled amidst splotches of light, creating an unusual amalgam of clarity and ambiguity.

"I find the pill to be a reliable form of contraception. I find condoms to be …stimulating."

A figure appeared, at first as a nebulous silhouette of a person floating from one side of the room to the other. As it settled next to a broad-armed chair, the figure became more defined, more real. Amy recognized him. Was it possible? No, it couldn't be. He was in the Caribbean, having a blast with his buddies and god knows who or what else.

"What do you find stimulating about condoms?"

Amy found herself drifting between the room she was in and the room she wished to be in. These were softball questions, easy enough for her mind to absorb as it wandered. What did they care if she roamed as she contemplated? She would appear to them as if deep in thought, searching for the truth. And that's if they were paying attention to her. Fuck them. There was something more compelling happening just past the hydrangeas, beyond the next tall sheet of glass.

"They make me think of his orgasm. They're tight to his cock for a reason, right? His dick smothered by his own come; it turns me on to visualize that. I enjoy unwrapping him after so I can watch, touch and lick all that naughtiness from his knob. It's almost as good as if he ..."

How could it be Dylan? He'd just texted her. He'd promised to call soon, said he missed her. He was out of the country, not in the next building. Focus Amy, focus. She'd mapped that body of his with her eyes and hands too many times to not recognize it, to not be able to distinguish it from some other man's body.

"...comes on me or on himself. That's like the original form of birth control, right? Something about all his jizz shooting in uncontrollable spurts, making a delicious little mess. If it were reliable, that would be my preference."

Look at his face, Amy. It's different. It's not Dylan. And he's wearing a tie. Dylan doesn't even own a tie.

"Amy, is something wrong?"

He's taking off his tie now, unwrapping himself from his day of work. Who is this? He's so familiar.

"No. I'm good. Did I miss something?"

36

"You seemed to be somewhere else for a moment. Let me ask you ..."

Sociology 3435, the sociology of gender—that's how Amy knew him. He was her TA last semester. How could it have taken her so long to place him? He was Dylan's doppelganger, for god's sake, her only reason for attending the mind-numbing 8:00 class every morning. He was also the reason she'd sat in the second row, just far enough from him to be inconspicuous, yet close enough to draw the distinctions between him and Dylan.

She was still assessing, still comparing. And he was making it easy. He hadn't stopped with his tie. He was stripping: one starchy, long-sleeved button-down, one pair of gray chinos. Was he taking off his clothes for her? Maybe, maybe not. He could see her, right? How could he not notice the girl across the courtyard—the bored one looking for trouble—the girl on the prowl.

"Amy? Are you with us?"

They couldn't see what she could see, could they? From Brooke and Jeremy's side of the table, it would be just an empty room flanking a common garden, not a room filled with promise.

"Of course. You were going to ask me?"

"What qualities do you look for in a partner?" Brooke asked.

"Qualities? Are you referring to disposition? Or character?"

"Up to you."

"Let me think about that for a minute." Or maybe she'd take two minutes—but not to mull over the question. A second after it had left Brooke's lips, she could have spit out her reply. No, she needed the time to contemplate other, more thorny questions. It was okay for her to gaze across the courtyard; after all, she was supposed to be considering and evaluating the perfect response.

He was down to his boxers. Why? Why would her teacher be stripping for her? Maybe he wasn't. Maybe there was someone else in the room, someone just out of sight, someone he was about to fuck. Where was she? Was she undressing as well? Why wasn't she helping him out of his shorts, tugging them to the floor so she, so everyone, could peer at his prick as it sprang free?

"I like quiet men, low-key men, men who don't have to shout to get my attention."

He's reaching for something on the floor, but what? It's a satchel, or some kind of briefcase, filled with clothes. So, he's changing, that's all. There's no girl secreted in the corner, wet with anticipation. She won't be tugging at his boxers, but neither will he.

He's probably going somewhere, and he didn't want to wear his tie. It must be confining for him, like wearing a knotted rope around his neck. What's he going to put on? What makes him comfortable?

"What is it about a quiet man that appeals to you?"

"They're sexy, right? I think there's a certain strength about them, a restrained confidence that I find attractive."

"So, a quiet confidence then?"

"Yeah. If I'm going to be in a relationship, one that lasts, it's important to me. And it can't be fake confidence either. I see that a lot."

"What do you mean?"

"Have you ever really liked someone? You know, you've reached a certain comfort level with them, let them into your life, everything's peaches and cream? And then, out of the blue, you learn who they really are. They'll say one thing that you never expected them to say, just one thing that they should have said back when they were pretending to be self-assured; and you're like, no, 'I can't respect you anymore.' It could be something as inane as, 'The smell of chocolate makes me nauseous' or something significant, like some wild-ass opinion on abortion. And then it's over, all that time wasted with someone you didn't really know."

"So when do you know they're the real thing? How long does that take?"

What's that in his hands? It looks like a pair of shorts and, what, a hoodie? He's going for a run or maybe to the gym. Yeah, they're running shorts. That's what he's up to. But why is he changing in the middle of a public room? Is it a teachers' lounge? Is it a men's lounge? And now he's reaching back into his satchel for something else. He's got a handful of some kind of black stretchy material. Compression shorts, I think. He's stepping out of his boxers. Oh shit, he's naked, isn't he? Look away! No, don't look away! It's Dylan's body, right? Same as looking at Dylan, right? Is it? Are you sure?

"It's not always a matter of time. I know when I look at a chair where he's sat, or a bed where he's slept or a space on the floor where I remember him standing and I see him, feel him there. That's when I know."

Turn from the window, that's it. You can't see me now, can you? I can see you, though. I can see your ass—Dylan's ass—same thing. It's tight and round. I like. You run a lot, don't you? So does Dylan. Don't pull up those compression shorts. Not yet. Turn around first. C'mon.

"Thank you, Amy," Jeremy said, nodding at Brooke as if acknowledging her perfect follow-up questions. "Would you like to take a short break? We've kept you in that chair the longest time. Perhaps stretch your legs a little?"

"No thanks, I'm good."

Just give me a peek, let me see what you've got. Nobody's looking at me now, not even you. That's it—hike up those shorts, slowly—there we go. There it is. Are you fucking kidding me? Your cock looks just like Dylan's. That's not supposed to happen. I've never seen two alike. What's going on here? Who set you up to do this to me? I

M.L. Joslyn

know your body, but I barely know you. Is this awkward? Am I supposed to look or not? It's okay if you see me now. I want you to know that your body, your flawless, firm body, captivates me. I want you to see that I'm interested. Why aren't your shorts up by now? You like your cock too, huh? Are you going to touch it, play with it? It's thick and just the right length. You've been told that before, haven't you? I bet you have. I tell Dylan all the time. I can't help it. I want you to know I like your cock. Maybe I could play with it later. Maybe you could play with it for me now. C'mon, wrap your fingers around it and tug, baby. Jerk it for me. Hold your balls in one hand and your cock in the other and have at yourself. I can't touch you now, but maybe later. Maybe if you play your cards right, I'll show you what I can do with that dick of yours. I don't have to guess; I touch it every day, one just like it. I hold it, I lift it, I feel it, I control it and I …have it—every morning, every night.

No, leave those shorts just where they are. I'm not done violating your right to privacy. Like you care. You wouldn't be naked in that big, open room if you cared. You want me to see. You want me to fuck you too, don't you?

Get yourself hard for me, Mr. TA. Stroke yourself while you stare across the courtyard. Make yourself ready, because I am. Ooh, yeah, nice, very nice. Keep going. Come kiss me. Undress me and then kiss me all over. Start wherever you want, but finish where I tell you. See how wet I am for you? You're a perfect fit. I know. I've had you before, and I'm going to have you again. Just give me a sign and I'm there.

"Amy? Brooke and I need a moment to go over some notes with each other. You're welcome to stay where you are; or if you want to get up and stretch for a minute, we'll come find you."

The yellowish-white glow was gone, as was the TA. He packed up and left …for his run, most likely. Where else would he have gone? To look for me? Will you return to change back into your tie? Maybe your timing will be perfect, and I'll be done playing with your colleagues. I'll be ready for you. I'm available tonight. I hope you're interested. I am.

Chapter Six

Amy approached the tall window with caution, heedful of the stage she was ascending, mindful of exposing herself as someone else's curiosity. She wanted a closer look at the room across the courtyard, hoping to better understand its purpose. If she could calculate its potential for yielding another engaging, stimulating performance, even better.

Brooke and Jeremy had sent her off to recess but hadn't supplied her with a key to the playground; she could only regard it from inside her bubble. The room looked much the same from this distance as it did from her chair. But now it was lifeless, uninhabited, dispiriting.

A quick glance at Brooke, and Amy knew she had some more time to kill. Since there was no better time killer than her smart phone, she trekked back to her purse and started digging. Sure enough, the gaudy-green alert light was blinking.

"Okay," Jeremy declared without a trace of weariness in his voice, "are we ready to continue?"

"Sure. Can I just check this message quickly? Sorry."

It was Dylan again. Another text, this time accompanied by a photograph. "Hope your interview went well! Sorry, had no idea. Anyway, thought you should see this." It was just a tiny thumbnail of a picture, too small for Amy to understand. She ran a finger across the screen, sort of hoping the photo would open, sort of hoping it would retreat back to the cloud as if it had never been sent.

What the hell? It took Amy a few seconds to comprehend the enlarged image she'd vacantly summoned and that now filled the screen of her phone. It was of a nicely furnished hotel room, dressed up in its decadent best. There were no people in the photograph; but if the strategically placed clusters of liquor bottles and abundance of festively licentious décor were any indication, a hell of a party was about to break out.

A bachelor party, Amy quickly decided. Aside from unexpected scatterings of decorative balloon bouquets, the room seemed to have been thoughtfully orchestrated to encourage the consumption of all things depraved or otherwise prohibited by the wives and girlfriends who would not be in attendance.

Amy wasn't sure why Dylan wanted her to see this picture. Was his intention to taunt? Was it to flaunt his imminent infidelity? Either way, she refused to allow it to ruffle her self-esteem any further. She had other, more important things on her mind and her own fling to arrange. Amy nodded at Jeremy, prodding him with a tacit gesture to move things along.

"In a typical week, how many times would you say you engage in sexual intercourse?"

"A typical week, huh? Hmm …I guess somewhere around a dozen or so times. It depends. But I may not have another typical week, ever."

"And for what length of time have you been having intercourse twelve times a week?"

"A year? Yeah, it's been about a year." Amy glanced over at Brooke, who wore a poorly-muffled expression of surprise, incredulity, jealousy or, more precisely, a patchwork blend of all three.

Once again the begging, blinking green light on Amy's phone grabbed her attention, a signal that someone somewhere was thinking about her. It was also a belated reminder that she had forgotten to stash it back into her purse. She cupped her phone deep in her palms, wanting to blot out the telltale pink plastic cover from Brooke and Jeremy's view, and casually opened the message: *"Wish you were here."*

M.L. Joslyn

A second later another text hit the screen: *"No, I'm not drunk."*

Yeah, right, Amy thought. Send me another picture of the room as it looks now. Let me count the guests and empty bottles littering up the background.

Without hesitation, Amy scrolled back to the picture Dylan had sent earlier, thinking she'd delete it but wanting to analyze it one more time. The balloons—they were so out of place. They didn't really fit into the otherwise quintessential stag party ambience.

Pressing two fingers against the screen, Amy enlarged the photo for a better look. She continued to magnify the picture until she'd figured it out. They weren't balloon bouquets; they were condom bouquets. The gold and blue puffed-up sheaths were tacky and distasteful but could be justified as event-appropriate. She quickly removed the image from her phone's memory, wishing she could erase it from hers as well.

"Have you ever had sexual intercourse on a first date?" Brooke's brows arched high as she reached for her dreary black handbag and plopped it onto her lap.

"Once."

Brooke sifted through the contents of her uninspiring purse, appearing irritated and lost. Amy and Jeremy couldn't help but follow her aberrant behavior with cocked heads and puzzled eyes. After a minute, the grimace of frustration that had gripped Brooke's face flipped to a triumphant smile. She had tracked down the prize she'd been searching for and had it in her grasp.

"And?"

"And what? It was just one time. I've had plenty of first dates, but only one of them ended with me getting laid."

"Did you have a second date with this fellow?"

Fellow? How old was Brooke, anyway? And what the fuck did it matter? "Yeah, I had a second date with that fellow."

Subject X

Amy didn't feel like discussing the details—not now, not today. And besides, Brooke didn't even appear to be listening. Her focus was elsewhere, on the short white tube she clutched in her palm.

"Did you have sexual intercourse with him a second time? It needn't have been on the second date."

"Yes, and a third time and a fourth time, and on and on." Amy really didn't want to go down that road, didn't want to think about it, or him. She was still in a relationship, albeit a precarious, teetering one, with this particular ...fellow.

Both Amy and Jeremy waited for Brooke to follow-up with another question or at least one of her drenched-in-poorly-veiled-smugness affirmations.

Instead, they watched her apply a ruby shade of gloss to her lips, as if she were preparing to ditch this mess of an interview and move on with her day.

That was a fine idea, as far as Amy was concerned. She had better things to do than diagram her sex life for these people, and she had better things to think about than her past or current relationships. Still, it seemed an odd time for Brooke to be working on her appearance.

After a minute or so of flagrant preening, Brooke continued, "So, this man very quickly established himself as a catch?"

"Yes, very quickly."

"Could you recall for me a quality or mannerism of his that put you so at ease?"

"I had met him once before, briefly. He was a ...gentleman." Amy didn't want to go any further with this. She'd already told Brooke and Jeremy the story of Dylan and how he'd come to her rescue in the fraternity house. She'd already told them he'd seen her naked. That was how they met; that was his first impression of her, the emotionally walloped nude girl.

M.L. Joslyn

***

"It's not fair, Dylan. You've already seen me without my clothes."

"Actually that would have been rude of me, Amy. I was just looking into your eyes, that's all."

"You're full of crap."

"Are you calling me a liar?"

"I'm just saying you're full of crap."

"Okay, I kind of peeked a little—twice—but not because I had any intention of being disrespectful. I couldn't help it. I'd caught just enough of a glimpse to see how pretty you were. I needed, I mean I had to have another look. Forgive me?"

"I don't know. It's still not fair."

"What are you saying? You want to see me naked?"

"Yeah. That's what I'm saying. It would make us even."

"Come with me," Dylan whispered, reaching for Amy's hand.

Dylan led Amy to his bedroom, which was just five steps from the den/kitchen/only other room in his apartment and barely six steps from the small, green fabric couch that had coaxed them to this moment with its scale of intimacy.

He was a stranger—kind of—yet here she was, falling with casual nonchalance atop his neatly-dressed twin bed, pulling him down next to her. They were both fully clothed; but as they embraced, they brushed aside any concern of wrinkled blouses or crumpled pants. It was time to focus on details only available at this range.

"You're so warm, Dylan."

His arms were around her, his fingers teasing the recessed stretch of her spine, up and down, across and over. Their eyes danced in unison, bright, eager puddles of curiosity and fascination.

"And you're so pretty, Amy."

46

He pulled away just a bit, sliding his arms from her back so he could rest his hand on a propped-up palm. He gazed at her as if she were a prize, his prize, a treat he hadn't expected—a wrapped present he wanted to relish.

Amy reached for the top button of his dusky gray cotton shirt and rolled it between her fingers. Dylan didn't say a word. She could move forward if she wanted; his eyes said so.

She squeezed the button through a split of fabric, exposing a sliver of smooth chest and a hint of gym-conditioned pecs. She palmed the firm slopes that rose beneath the cloaking spread of cloth—but it wasn't enough. She wanted more, reached for a second button and then a third. Finally she could slide her hands across his skin, feeling, learning the turns and bends that she'd only imagined but hadn't had the chance to understand.

His turn. He made that decision before she did. Amy's blouse was easier: no buttons for his long, thick fingers to bargain with, no stiff fabric for them to skirmish against.

He dispatched her silky blouse with relative ease and then her stiff, complex bra as if it were scarcely a challenge. His hand edged behind her short, flared black skirt; and he released the snared button, eliminating a potential obstacle. He left the skirt in place, not saying a word, but with a tacit promise to deal with it later.

With noses brushing, Dylan placed a soft kiss along a corner of Amy's bottom lip, savoring the surge of intimacy, searching for any sign of resistance. She responded with like interest, her lips parting, exhorting him to pursue his curiosity.

He kissed the ridge of her shoulder next, then her chin and then the warm, soft crook in between. She purred in response, drawing deep breaths of musk, dark chocolate and Cashmere wood.

But he didn't linger, didn't outstay his welcome. Instead,

he advanced south to the small, firm globes he'd been itching to caress and yearning to taste. His moist tongue flicked at a stiffening nipple before drawing it into his mouth, sucking it, bathing it further.

Amy whimpered as Dylan sought nourishment from every exposed inch of her. He nuzzled and kissed the soft bottoms of her receptive tits, then shifted to the long smooth arc between her neck and waist. She wanted him naked and she wanted him on his back so she could pleasure him as well, but he wasn't done exploring or tasting.

Amy didn't quibble, nor did she offer assistance as Dylan slid her unfastened skirt over her feet, tossing it onto an overstuffed corduroy pillow that had tumbled from the bed. He was on his knees, between her legs, drinking in everything he'd purposely, respectfully avoided the day they'd met, the day he wasn't supposed to be looking. But today was a different story, a different Dylan and a different Amy.

She watched his eyes scan her body, tracing her curves as if he were searching for a way in—or maybe he was plotting his way in—she wasn't sure. His shirt was off, but his pants still clung to his thighs, waist and the seemingly endless span of his powerful, reaching cock.

"What are you waiting for?" Amy didn't intend for the words to spill from her mouth, but her needs were too overwhelming and the question too powerful for her to contain.

"Shhh …we have time."

Dylan's hands slithered from Amy's knees to her thighs, over silky skin and toned muscle, until they reached the thin elastic waistband of her panties. His fingers stretched under the fabric, feeling, rubbing her creamiest, most secret spread of skin. His hands circled her split cautiously, skirting her core of heat and dampness, savoring the landscape.

With fingers curled over the top of her thong, he slowly

began to pull. Amy grabbed his wrists, quickly shifting control to her corner.

"Not until those clothes come off."

He smiled but did not speak a word. It was their first date but already Amy could read the man, know his thoughts without hearing them. He'd remove his pants and boxers; that wouldn't be a problem. He wanted her and he would obey her commands. Whatever it would take to have her, to move along with his plan, that's what he was thinking, what he'd be saying—if words were necessary.

"You'll have to let go of my arms—just for a moment."

He was still on his knees, between her legs. When she let her hands fall to the bed, he stood, a towering presence, half-cloaked, all-primed.

His pants descended easily. Amy wasn't watching as he kicked them to the floor or as they landed in a twisted coil atop her skirt. Her focus was elsewhere, on the man peering down at her with lust in his eyes—on the man whose hand was reaching into his boxers.

"Do you need some help?" Amy wasn't sure why he was grabbing his cock. Wasn't that her role? Hadn't she earned the right?

"No thanks. Just give me a sec."

Amy understood quickly. He wasn't able to slide his shorts off as effortlessly as his pants. There was something holding them up, something wedged fast against the knit fabric, something hindering their removal. That's why his hands were holding his cock against his belly, so he could slide his shorts down his legs. And that's when she got to see him—all of him—for the first time.

"Wait." Amy spoke too late. He was already crouched on his knees, his hands mingling with her panties. She'd only gotten a cursory look at him, at the parts she didn't know, the parts she wouldn't be able to single out in a lineup. She had wanted to sit up but he'd paralyzed her, knocked her to a

M.L. Joslyn

powerless, vulnerable state. She had melted into the cradling caress of a fresh-scented pillow and fleecy blanket, yet she was privately, secretly, feeling more alive than ever.

His kisses started just above her knees, soft, warm trails of them that seemed to linger long after his lips had moved on. Her fingers stretched to find dense twists of his tousled hair, and she combed through it, her nails grazing, massaging his scalp as he inched his way north.

With a hand on each of Amy's thighs, Dylan gently, but insistently, coaxed them apart. His kisses deepened, became something more than a brush of lips against skin. He was …tasting her, she thought.

The higher Dylan climbed, the more he became consumed with her smoothness, her strength, her flirtatious, aromatic scent.

When his tongue met her pussy, she was beyond ready. The tip knocked at her slim, dewy lips, nudging them slightly, urging them further apart. He drew a single lip into his mouth and she shuddered, her ass lifting from the blanket, his tongue staying with her, persistent, hungry.

Dylan's hands moved to grab her vulnerable, available ass, and he held tight, squeezing, kneading her soft cheeks. He lapped at her and fawned over her—until her whimpers grew to shrieks—until he caught flashes of orgasm in her eyes and in his mouth.

Amy grabbed at his hair, his face, his shoulders, any part of him she could, using what remaining strength she had to pull him on top of her. She was desperate to feel his strong, warm body cover her and enter her.

She was so close to making it happen, so close to guiding him home. She urgently needed to be filled, and he had what she needed. She'd yet to touch his thick, stiff cock—had only been offered a fleeting glimpse of it. And though she'd blindly gauged its dimensions, its heft, as it inadvertently, fortuitously pressed against the smoothness of her calf, it was

50

only part of what she desired. She wanted Dylan, not just pieces of him. He wasn't merely a first date. She couldn't explain it, even to herself.

But before their lips could meet, before she could feel the flutter of his lashes against her cheeks and before he cast the first inch of himself into her soul, he stopped ascending. How disrespectful of him to challenge her efforts and her strength.

What was he doing worshipping her body this way? She was ready for him, and she wanted him—now. But she couldn't complain, wouldn't spill a scornful word his way. No, as much as she wanted him inside her and as eager as she was to experience him, every fucking inch of him, he was still making love to her, still devouring her.

At first it was a nipple, just a nipple. He sucked on it gently, pausing only to roll his tongue, briefly, around the sensitive circle of skin that surrounded it. Then back to the nipple again, until finally his mouth unhinged. He bathed her breast with his tongue as he drew it in, and he showered it with kisses as it slipped away. Back and forth, back and forth, her tit was fucking his mouth. Her other breast was fully in his grasp, encompassed by his broad palm and stroked by his lustful fingers.

Dylan shifted position, his mouth and fingers trading places as if demanding equal time ...and pleasure. Amy stopped him.

"Now." Although it quivered as it spilled from her lips, Amy spoke the word clearly and convincingly. Dylan wouldn't need to hear it twice.

She reached for his cock to usher him in and to touch it for the first time. If she couldn't see it with her eyes, she would at least see it through her fingers. He was halfway in before her fingers had a chance.

It didn't matter. She didn't need eyes or fingers anymore. She didn't care. She had what she'd been craving. And he was everything she'd hoped: strong, yet gentle, weighty and yet comforting. She could see him later, all of him. And then she'd see him again, and then again.

It was only a first date, and Amy understood quite well that people are not always who they at first seem to be. She'd been down those roads, fallen for those façades and tripped over those wires. Her instincts had failed her before, but there was something about Dylan—something different—something good.

Both of them were spent, and Dylan was unable, or unwilling, to speak. With his arms still wrapped around her, his cock reluctantly retreating from her pussy, he rolled them onto their sides so they could face each other, maybe read each other's thoughts. Amy searched his eyes to see if he could tell what she was thinking. She wanted him to know; she wanted to just blurt it out so she could gauge his response. But it was too soon. She knew better. She also knew that if it were up to her, this would be the last first date of her life.

Chapter Seven

"Have you ever utilized more than one position for sexual intercourse?" Brooke shot a sideways glance toward Jeremy, as if seeking his endorsement of her question.

"You mean, have I ever changed positions while I'm fucking someone?"

"Actually I'm asking if you've ever tried more than one position for intercourse."

"Seriously? Are there people that have only screwed one way? That would be pretty boring, huh?"

"So, I take that as a 'yes'. Now, of the positions you've tried, do you have a favorite? Hmm?"

Jeremy had been fighting the distraction of Brooke's evolving persona. He wasn't sure what she was up to, or why she had discarded the blatantly inadequate map they had charted. Was she attempting to coax deeper responses from Amy by engaging in some sort of behavior modification scheme? Was she hoping to redefine the status of her relationship with the girl?

Jeremy was supposed to be noting Amy's subconscious gestures and tics as she absorbed their questions and formulated her responses. He had been trained to identify telling, subtle signs of deception or candidness. He'd take his notes, he'd listen to the tapes with Brooke and then they would piece together an accurate analysis of the interview. He hadn't counted on having to pay attention to his cohort's mutating guise.

"Um, I really have never tried anything …objectionable. A favorite? I suppose any position where I can see more of him, you know?"

"So, there are no positions you find distasteful or unacceptable?"

Jeremy found Brooke's questions, the ones that had begun frolicking from her lips with more of a busybody edge than an investigative edge, amusing as well as distracting. For some reason, she had refashioned herself from a thesis-focused grad student to a riveted, gossipy girlfriend the moment she had learned of Amy's exceptionally active sex life. She was still phrasing her questions the same; but she'd restyled her voice, pitching it higher and friendlier. Her eyes had brightened too, from dispassionate puddles of stale cobalt safeguarded behind thick glasses to fiery pools of shameless sapphire.

And then there was Brooke's sudden quest for attention. Jeremy wondered why she had decided to apply lip gloss in the midst of an interview—red lip gloss. Was it an intentional gambit designed to narrow the dissimilarities between her and Amy? Was she hoping they could become friends?

"I don't know that I would find every position acceptable. It's not like I've attempted the entire *Kama Sutra*."

It was right after she asked Amy about having sex on a first date. Jeremy remembered that that's when Brooke had fumbled through her purse for the tube of gloss. What was it about that question?

Ten minutes earlier, Jeremy would have bet the house that Brooke had never screwed on a first date. He pictured her as the disengaged scientist, exempt from needing sex at all. And on a first date? Not worth the risk—emotionally or physically.

But now? He wasn't so sure. She'd been exhibiting a bit of a talent for role-playing. Maybe she'd give it a go on a whim perhaps or out of professional curiosity.

"Are you comfortable receiving oral sex from your partners?"

Jeremy glanced at Brooke, almost certain he'd seen her wink at Amy from the corner of his eye, wondering if she'd do it again. He wouldn't put it past her, despite the red flags of impropriety such a move would raise. She had become an enigma to him. She had also become much more intriguing.

Would she fuck him on their first date? Jeremy struggled to scrub the question from his head as he mentally undressed her. A date? With Brooke? Did she date men? Did she even like men? Would he actually date her?

Stop it, Jeremy! Stop it! The words pounded through his head with insistent fury. First it was Amy—hot little Amy with her short skirt and clingy sweater. Now it was Brooke with her heavy wool blazer and indecipherable curves. They both excited him, and that wasn't supposed to happen. They were both messing with his head, and it had to stop—or else. *Or else what, Jeremy? No more grad school? No more future as a social scientist? Would he forever be cast as a mad scientist?*

"Comfortable? Having someone give me oral sex? Seriously? A warm tongue on my pussy—it's kind of hard to top that sensation, right? Mmm. I mean there are a couple things that might. Or maybe there's just one thing. I'd have to think about that."

What the fuck *was* under that intolerably frumpy blazer of hers? Jeremy had to know. There was a scoop neck blouse for starters. What did that mean? Why would a woman pair a heavy jacket with a thin, low-cut blouse? She was protecting herself and exposing herself at the same time, as if she were standing nude in a dark body of water.

That was it, Jeremy decided. He had to stop right where he was before he undressed her further. It wasn't too late. He just had to focus his attention elsewhere.

"So, Brooke, if you don't mind, I have some questions for Amy."

Brooke sat back in her chair and thrust one leg across the other, nodding as she passed the baton to Jeremy.

"What part of the day do you prefer for intercourse?

Morning? Evening? Sometime in between?" Jeremy hoped his spiceless question would douse the snowballing desire he had of figuratively or, if he were looking for trouble, literally uncloaking the girls.

"I don't really pay attention to what time it is. For me, sex feels best when we both want it. It could be the middle of the day or the middle of the night. It really doesn't matter."

Amy glanced at her watch as if to validate her response, then stole a peek at the room across the courtyard. The afternoon was slipping away, and she was a minute closer to wrapping up this increasingly inane survey. She was also a minute closer to unwrapping an increasingly needed, sensible man. She just needed to find one.

The room was still empty. Her TA had yet to return for her. Maybe he was still jogging around campus, formulating a plan to ask her out. Maybe he'd want to screw her lights out, then take her to some cozy Italian bistro for a bite after. Or maybe he was a middle-of-the-night guy. Maybe he didn't like to have sex before dinner.

She needed a backup plan. Mr. TA couldn't be counted on to return. Even if he did, he might not be interested. Maybe she wasn't his type. He might prefer curves, or blondes, or big tits. Anyway, he could very well be off the market, already settled into an honest relationship with a faithful partner. That's right, lots of couples were faithful to one another. It was possible.

What time was it in the Bahamas? It was the same time as in Columbus, day tapering to evening. And with the withering sunlight came the promise of nightfall and all the transgressions it might conceal. Dylan had already attended one party. He was probably getting ready for another— unless he'd already found his distraction for the day.

Dylan was a middle-of-the-day kind of guy. Shit, he was an any-time-of-day kind of guy. Go ahead, Dylan. Send me a picture email of what you've been doing this afternoon—of your hot little D cup transgression.

"Are you as orgasmic in the middle of the afternoon as you are in the middle of the night, then?"

"Yeah, um …" Amy had a sudden urge to look at the picture again, the one Dylan had sent of the party room. Maybe she hadn't looked close enough before. Maybe the lucky bitch was somewhere in the background, plugging in her cheap boom box or slipping into her slutty come-fuck-me heels. *What does she look like, Dylan? What is it I'm missing that she's got?*

Fuck! As Amy reached for her phone, she realized she'd erased the picture earlier. She'd been fuming over the classic stag party backdrop and had no need to see the rows of neatly-stacked shot glasses or the tables dressed with bouquets of condom balloons.

The condom balloons—was it possible? Were they Dylan's? Is that why he'd packed boxes of them—for decorations?

"Why would I be any less orgasmic at three in the afternoon? I wouldn't have sex if I didn't want to have sex. Doesn't matter what time it is."

Those fucking condoms weren't *fucking* condoms; they were stupid bachelor-party- centerpiece condoms. Amy's skin dampened and her cheeks flushed as she realized that she'd misinterpreted Dylan's plan for the prophylactics. She wasn't embarrassed; she was pissed—at herself—and at Dylan. Why hadn't he explained them away? Because she hadn't given him the chance, that's why. There were so many of them. It should have registered; she should have known.

But …maybe not all of the condoms had been used for décor. Maybe he had a box of them stashed away for his own use. She would never know. She could only assume.

"What sort of setting do you prefer for sex? A dark secured room, a middle seat on a commercial airliner or something in between?"

"Wow, I guess I really don't care. I would say I'm definitely not an active exhibitionist, you know, someone who wants or needs other people to watch."

"Would you get a rush of excitement if you thought a stranger were spying your naked body?"

"I suppose modesty used to be more important to me than it is now. I mean I don't know why anyone would want to see me without clothes. But my pussy's been on display, remember? And strangers have seen my tits. Kind of water under the bridge, right? The truth is, I've only been with two guys who would screw somewhere in public. One of them was my first, who I only had sex with once. The other guy is—or was, sorry—always wanting to experiment, always looking to make everything as much fun as ...possible."

***

"I have to tell you, Dylan. I haven't been to this beach since I was a little girl. It's actually a lot nicer than I recall. The sand's so white and soft."

"I know. For Lake Erie, it's not bad at all. Thanks for agreeing to the trip and for packing your bathing suit. I promise I just want to hang out on the beach for a little bit, and then we can hit the rides. Okay?"

"Okay, but it's Cedar Point. There's like sixteen roller coasters here. I can hear them. I can see them. I want to ride them!"

"Sure, sweetie. Don't worry; we'll get to spend almost the whole day inside the park. I'll even buy you a cotton candy. You like cotton candy?"

"I'm not five, Dylan. I'm not going to start crying if we can't go on the rides yet. But yes, I like cotton candy. Can I get a swirly pink and blue flavored one?"

"I'm pretty sure pink and blue aren't flavors, but yeah! We're here to have fun, and we can do whatever you want.

And, by the way, I know you're not a child. You are a very delectable young lady. There's no doubt in my mind. And based on the stares you've been getting from every man passing by, I'm not the only one who appreciates your hotness."

"My hotness? You're funny. I'm not so sure you're right about that, but thanks."

"Seriously. You are so sexy in that bikini. What sort of material is this, spandex or something?"

"Dylan, shhh …I know we're outside, but maybe you should be using your inside voice. This beach is really crowded. And yeah, it's probably at least part spandex; and no, you can't keep touching it. Especially there."

"But this is where I want to touch it. And here too, and here."

"Dylan, cut it out. People are staring."

"How can you tell? Everyone's wearing sunglasses. But listen, before you get me any more turned-on, maybe we should take a dip in the lake."

"Eww. Really? It's Lake Erie. I don't think people are supposed to swim in it. I'm not even sure if fish swim in it."

"Now you're just being goofy, Amy. Look at all the people out there. The water is perfectly clean and safe. I promise you'll have fun. Okay? C'mon, get up. Here—grab my hand."

Amy watched her boyfriend jump to his feet and swat sand off his crisp, navy blue trunks with his free hand. But she was unwilling to budge. She'd let him scoop her off her pink and yellow striped beach towel in a minute, after she'd soaked in enough of him to flood the corners of her greedy mind. She liked this view of him, this perspective from the sand, the way his broad shadow swallowed her, cooled her off and heated her up all at the same time.

As Dylan leaned over her, a vision of tousled, sun-blanched hair and begging, clear brown eyes, she smiled. He was perfect, too perfect; always fun, always thoughtful, always the gentleman – always the cutest guy in the room.

And here he was, calling her sexy, reaching for her hand. He said she was turning him on, but it was mutual. She was getting wet but had yet to dip a toe in the water.

"Okay, Dylan. You win." Wearing a yielding smirk, Amy allowed Dylan to lift her from the beach and into his arms.

"Of course I win. I'm here with you! C'mon!" Dylan trotted into the lake, holding tightly to Amy's hand. Flaunting his boyish charm, he splashed through the water with excessive enthusiasm. It did nothing to quell Amy's resistance. "See? The water's pretty clear, and it's even kind of warm."

"There are like hundreds of tiny fish swimming past our legs, Dylan. I will scream if even one of them bites me."

"Like this?"

"Mmm …that's a nibble, not a bite. And I was talking about them biting my legs. I don't think these fish could jump high enough to reach my neck."

"Don't be surprised—the water's over your waist. Hey, you know what I love about this? I can touch my little Amy here, and even here, and nobody can see what I'm doing."

"Your little Amy? Am I just another one of your …things?"

"Nope. But these are!"

"Dylan! Cut it out! There are people everywhere!"

"And they're not paying a bit of attention to us. Are you telling me you don't want me to play with your tits?"

"Yes! That's what I'm telling you."

"Then maybe I'll find something else to play with …like this! Ooh, you're all wet."

"Very funny, Dylan. Now get your fucking fingers out of there."

"My fucking fingers, huh? Hey, that's a great idea. Thanks."

"What the …?"

"Shhh …nobody can see what I'm doing. Just relax! Doesn't this feel good?"

"Um, hmm. Yeah, it feels good. But …"

"Ooh, yeah, thanks for reminding me. Can't forget your butt!"

"Dylan! Get your finger out of …"

"Shhh, Amy. You're talking too much. Wrap your arms around my neck. I'll take us into deeper water."

"Shit, you're really doing a number on me—mmm …oh boy. Um, but if I wrap both my hands around your neck, I won't be able to check out what you've got going down here. Whoa …you are really hard, Dylan. So, what are you thinking?"

"I stopped thinking a minute ago, Amy. C'mon, let's get a little deeper into the lake."

"I kind of like it right here. Could you …would you give me a sec to pull off my bottoms?"

"Really? You are not only the prettiest girl on this beach, you're also the coolest."

"Yeah …thanks—oh god, does that feel good—but, hmmm, I'd also like to be the most comfortable."

"Let me help. My hands are already here. In fact, I need to get my hair wet anyway."

"Dylan!" Amy looked around to see if anyone heard her screeching out her boyfriend's name or if anyone had noticed that he'd suddenly, mysteriously disappeared.

From Amy's perspective, Dylan might have been a mirage: a whorl of soft, indistinct patterns dancing below the water's surface, begging contemplation. But she knew who he was and what he was trying to do; in fact, she was helping him do it.

At a plodding, water-thwarted tempo, Amy narrowed her stance so her bikini bottom could slide down easier, and then, once it was in Dylan's hands, widened it so he could

M.L. Joslyn

access what he had been straining to access. Demonstrating uncharted levels of self-control, she remained silent, hopeful that her boyfriend's breath would hold for one, maybe two more passes of his tongue.

His lungs depleted, Dylan nuzzled his way up Amy's body, ascending beyond her blissfully-parted split to the sweep of her supple belly. He pressed on, skimming the arc of her barely-concealed breasts with his cheeks and acknowledging their allure with quick, furtive nibbles. He framed her flushed face between his palms and began kissing her gently, sampling her full lips between his, nudging them apart until she invited him in.

"Wrap your legs around my waist, Amy. Don't worry— I've got you." Dylan whispered the words in her ear, his warm breath and shameless enthusiasm caressing her like an anxious finger on a loaded gun.

Doing her best to conceal the buzz charging through her body, Amy latched her face to Dylan's to prevent her passion from giving them away. With her arms linked tight around his neck, her scarcely veiled breasts pressed firmly against his well-defined bare chest and her feet knotted over his flexing ass, she drew in every inch of his thick, stiff prick.

Folded in Dylan's unyielding embrace, Amy lost herself in a circle of new and familiar sensations. They slow danced through the water, Dylan leading but Amy in control. His hands moved to her ass, kneading, squeezing, working her cheeks; but she was working his cock, discreetly thrusting her hips so he'd nudge her clit the way she liked and then thrust them again so he'd fill her pussy the way she liked. She didn't want to raise her head from the curve of his neck. She didn't need to see who was watching. She no longer cared.

"You are so fucking delicious," Dylan whispered over the rhythmic beat of lapping water.

"Oh god, Dylan, I'm coming," Amy whimpered to the

62

beads of spray atop his shoulder. "Fuck me hard and hold me tight. Don't let go. Don't let go."

"Babe, I'm there too. I'm with you. You are so sweet; I want every shred, every part of you. I can't get enough. I can't get …oh, Amy. Oh man. Oh."

For a few moments they remained as one, bobbing to the fading pulse of their orgasms. The chirpy sounds of the amusement park suddenly reappeared.

"Mmm. Pretty good idea you had, Dylan. Mmm. Fuck the roller coasters. I just went on the best ride in the park."

"I love you, Amy."

"I think you swallowed too much lake water, Dylan."

"Maybe. But that has nothing to do with how I feel about you. C'mon, let's dry off. I owe you a cotton candy."

Chapter Eight

"Amy, let's talk about masturbation for a moment." Brooke articulated her statement with a surprising lilt of informality, sat back in her chair and then brushed a pen against her lips.

"Go ahead." Amy wasn't sure why Brooke suddenly sounded like a sympathetic friend from a tampon commercial or why she wanted to talk about something rather than ask about something.

"How often?"

"As in how often do I need to service myself? Or do you mean how often do I enjoy getting myself off?"

"Answer how you'd like."

"I would say I enjoy getting off as much as possible. If I have to do myself, I don't mind at all. Nobody else knows my body better, right?"

"Could you quantify 'as much as possible' for me? Is that once a week? Once a day?"

"Yeah. I'm not on a schedule, you know? If I'm in a sexual relationship, I might play with myself less, I guess, or sometimes my partner turns me on so much that just thinking about him gives me the urge to, you know."

"What about pornography? Is that a stimulus for you?"

"Does it make me horny? Occasionally, I suppose. I actually find it more informative than arousing."

"Fingers or toys—which do you prefer?"

Jeremy glanced at his partner, careful to keep his emotional distance from her—not sure if he could. She'd been poking about Amy's nightstand drawer without giving the girl an opportunity to tour them around and expound on her answers. Brooke's hurried cadence smacked of desperation, as if her questions were driven by personal curiosity, as if she were exploiting their study to find holes in her own nightstand drawer.

"Depends on whether I want to really fuck myself or just play with myself. If I'm feeling a little …kinky, I guess, my fingers aren't going to do it for me. I mean they're a little too familiar, right? Not that I don't enjoy the occasional hand trip. Who doesn't?"

For a second Jeremy thought Brooke was preparing to answer Amy's rhetorical question. She wanted to, he could tell: the look in her eyes, the hesitancy to continue, and the way her hands danced in her lap. *Go ahead, Brooke. Tell Amy how you like to diddle yourself. Pretend I'm not here.*

Jeremy kept an eye on Brooke's hands, intrigued by their movement, the way they tripped over one another as they plucked at the thick weave of her skirt. He glanced at Amy, wanting to see what her hands were doing, wondering if they too were pawing at the fibers that covered her sex.

The dichotomy was glaring: Amy's short, slender skirt, fashioned from lightweight fabric and hemmed to seduce, versus Brooke's knee-length pocket protector of a skirt, starchy and dispassionate. Yet for some reason he found Brooke's garment as provocative and distracting as Amy's, perhaps because she was flirting with herself through the ponderous cloth, or perhaps because the object of her flirtation was so inaccessible.

"You imply that sometimes you feel a little kinky. Could you describe an act of kinky masturbation for us?"

"Um, well, I might have overstated that thought. I suppose in the grand scheme of things, my idea of kinkiness is probably pretty lame."

"Go on."

"Ok. Um, well, what the hell. I screwed a doorknob—once. Maybe the most awkward, unrewarding sex act I've ever pulled off, so to speak. I've also fucked a wall or I should say I occasionally fuck a wall. Technically, I guess,

M.L. Joslyn

it's a rubber penis that I suction-cup to the wall in my shower. Does that sound better? And, uh, let's see. Oh, this is a good example: One day last spring I was swimming laps at my apartment complex pool when I noticed one of my girlfriends catching some rays on a lounge chair. So I swim over, grab the edge of the deck with both hands and begin to catch up with her. Suddenly this hard stream of warm water starts pulsing from the wall I was pressed against. It was just an annoying blast of water at first, part of the filtering system for the pool, I guess. When I began to edge away from it, a surge of water pushed its way into my bikini top and flicked at my nipple. It was this driving, silky force that felt so, stimulating; it caught me totally by surprise. So, now I'm kind of turned-on, and I start moving around, searching for the perfect angle for the stream to frolic with my tits. I'm sure I looked like an idiot to my friend, but I couldn't help but play with this rush of water. It felt amazing."

"So, you're able to achieve orgasm by stimulating your breasts then."

"Wait, I'm not finished; yeah, they may be small, but they're very responsive. Anyway, my friend's chatting away, telling me about her Saturday night; and I'm smiling, pretending to be paying attention, when all I want to do is come, right? Like a total idiot, I hadn't even considered that this jet of water might be ten times more fun than any handheld showerhead I'd ever played with. So without wasting any more time, I grab the deck of the pool, spread my legs and plant my feet against the wall, edging them higher and higher till I reach the perfect position. As soon as I've got it locked in, I pull aside my bikini bottom and let the water charge into my pussy and flood my clit with its unrelenting blast of warmth. It was so overwhelming I came right away; and then, lined up right behind that orgasm, was another. It was amazing. I mean, I think I had tears in my eyes. Anyway, that probably doesn't qualify as kinky masturbation, since I've got to be the last girl in the pool to have figured that one out. The kinky part, I guess, was that I told my friend, who by now was perched at the edge of her lounge chair. I mean I couldn't keep it to myself, right? So she starts laughing and asks if I were serious about never having gotten off that way before, and did I not realize she was quite aware of what I was doing? Then she tells me that the pool pump always comes on this time of day, winks at me and asks how much longer I'll be. I don't know—that's kind of kinky, right?"

"Everyone's definition of 'kinky' is unique," Brooke replied, stealing a glance at Jeremy. She wished she could read his thoughts, hear his stories and listen to *his* definition of "kinky." But despite her desire to vacuum telling crumbs of carnal dirt from Jeremy's head, she was still busy distilling Amy's masturbation stories. In particular, Brooke was intrigued by the way Amy had introduced the concept of fucking a wall, the way she matter-of-factly mentioned that she occasionally does such a thing; it struck her right between her thighs.

Brooke had a shower too, a large one with a broad, tiled wall. How many of Amy's rubber dicks would fit along that wall, she wondered. Five? Ten? What would she do with all of them? They'd each be a unique size and shape, wouldn't they? Some thick and long, too hefty to stand at attention, some smaller that would arc up as if pleading to be fucked, and one of them …well, it would look like Jeremy's dick or at least as she imagined it to look. That would be the one she'd want right now, the one that would satisfy her the most. No. She'd do the rest of them first, saving his for last. She'd grab the first one in line and suck on it a little. Then she'd jerk the adjacent one with her tight fist while taking the following one deep and fast.

Eventually she'd reach him, the one she really wanted, the one she craved. She'd hold him with ten fingers, feeling his heft, waiting for his desire to match hers. He'd take her from behind, but tentatively, as if unsure how his actions might affect their professional alliance. But it wouldn't matter, not at all. She could set the pace, and she could tell him how to penetrate her. *That's right, Jeremy. Just like that. Yeah, that's how I want you to fuck me. I'm taking all of you now, every fucking inch of you. No, don't touch my back door, not yet. You can look at it, though, and you can dream of having it, someday maybe, but not now. All I want is to screw every drop of come from you. Give it to me, Jeremy. Give it to me.*

"Are you waiting for me to reply to that?" Amy asked, puzzled by Brooke's cloudy stare and the correspondent aura of discomforting stillness that surrounded it.

"Reply to what?" Brooke answered, unsure of where she had left off.

"You said everyone's definition of 'kinky' is unique. I don't disagree."

"Exactly. Let's continue. Do you ever masturbate with a partner, Amy?"

"Yeah, once in a while. Well, I've told you how much I enjoy watching a man come, so I suppose mutual masturbation is one way of ensuring I get my reward, right?"

"Where is your focus during this exercise?"

"I, um, why would you refer to making love as an exercise? I mean, even if I'm not touching him, it's still a position, right? We're still making love, not practicing for a piano recital. I don't mean to be …insolent, but haven't we reached the point where we can talk like real people?"

"There's a certain protocol," Jeremy jumped in, trying to prevent the train from derailing, afraid Brooke already had one wheel off the track, "that precludes us from leading you with potentially emotive language. And, by the way, we're appreciative of your candor. You're not being insolent. You're providing us with a special insight that's very beneficial to our study. Please understand."

"Alright. My focus, at least at first, is on his erection: the way it firms up, the way it reddens from the friction, the way it validates his lust for me. But I'm touching myself as well, right? So very quickly I'm having this mixed focus: his cock, my pussy, his eyes, all the while observing, feeling, waiting. I look for signs, careful to avoid my clit while I'm teasing the hell out of him—and while he's teasing the hell out of me. I could get myself off quickly, but that's not my objective. I want him to get off first. I don't want to be lost in my orgasm when he comes. I want to see his orgasm, you know? I want to feel the warm cream spot my breasts and drizzle down my thighs."

"So, your focus is on his impending orgasm?"

"Actually, no. I just don't want to miss it. I really get into watching him stroke himself. It turns me on—a lot."

"It gives you a sense of domination or control. Is that what turns you on?" Jeremy twisted in his seat as he asked.

"No. I mean, I never think of it that way. Maybe I'm just more easily aroused by erotic images than most girls. I don't want to visualize an erect penis as much as I want to see it. I don't know. Maybe I'm wrong. But just about everything I've read leads me to believe I'm kind of ...an oddity? Women want to think and feel. Men want to see. Tell me you don't enjoy the sight of jiggling tits, round butts or a beckoning set of moist lips. I'm right, aren't I? I think a nice bulge will turn most women on. I go for that as well. But a close look at a hard cock is what really does it for me." Amy's eyes locked with Jeremy's, daring him to blink first. "I don't consider that an example of being on some sort of power trip. I'm just a girl who appreciates a good visual."

Amy watched Jeremy fidget a bit, his hands working his thighs like a potter throwing clay on a wheel. He appeared to be fashioning a small plate—or perhaps a nut dish. Either way, he was obviously trying to conceal something from her, something he could no longer control.

M.L. Joslyn

Jeremy's presumptuous, yet perceptive assessment circled through her head. He seemed to think her desire to glare at men's cocks came from her need for control. Maybe he was right. Maybe he had experience, personal experience with girls like her. Maybe he liked girls who weren't afraid to grab the reins and insist—no, demand—a show, so they could see him come.

"What do you think about when you see a new partner's penis for the first time?" Brooke gazed at the empty space between Amy's chair and Jeremy's as she asked.

"Well, the first time they're always erect, aren't they?" Amy cast a glance at Jeremy, letting him know she was paying attention.

"These questions are for you to answer, not me, Amy," Brooke replied.

Amy wondered about that. It seemed Brooke and Jeremy had been clawing at her mind for more than just breezy answers or routine filler for their study. It was as if they were seeking confirmation or validation for their personal intimacy issues. How could she help them cope with their obvious insecurities? She had enough trouble handling her own.

"Okay, well, I guess I think about how it would fit in my mouth. Then I wonder how it would taste."

Maybe they want me for something else, Amy considered. Maybe they're just pretending to be doctoral candidates scrounging for dirt to fill their theses. They certainly had that bookish, scholarly look down to a tee, that oblivious-to-everything- that-mattered-to-the-rest-of-the-world look. The room? They could have rattled all the doorknobs along the hallway searching for one that was unoccupied, one that would complement their ambitious ruse.

"It's funny," Amy continued. "I don't think about how it would feel in my pussy, at least not at first. Maybe I should. I don't know."

70

Real grad students or not, there was something going on with these two that poked at the boundaries of acceptable behavior, Amy thought. They were too …affected by her responses.

"What size penis *do* you prefer?" Brooke asked, her lips twisted in a disconcerting half-smile, half-smirk curlicue.

Amy pondered the possibilities. What if Jeremy did want to have sex with her? Would she? Could he possibly be who *she* was looking for? It would be easy to make it happen, at least a lot easier than her other options. She'd have a difficult time scouting for her TA, the one from across the courtyard, the one with the hard body who had stripped down to nothing because he had wanted her, not because he had wanted to tease and then run off with some other girl. And what about Brooke? Did she want to take part too, or was she just trying to pre-qualify someone for Jeremy, her pal, her sometimes lover?

Where else would she find a partner for the evening anyway, a partner preloaded with every spec of information necessary to soothe all of her aches and press all of her buttons?

"What size penis do I prefer? Does it matter? If he's everything I want, are the dimensions of his dick that important?"

"Amy, please."

"Okay, my ideal penis. Hmm. I suppose the really big ones used to scare me. I mean I'm not that big a girl, and the thought of anything—" Amy's gaze scurried toward Jeremy's lap, gauged what he was hiding and with hands spaced appropriately held them high for Brooke to see—"this large, would turn me off more than turn me on. Then Dylan fell into my life. We screwed before I had a chance to see his erection. It wouldn't have mattered what it looked like; I just wanted him inside me— desperately. When I got my first eyeful of him, I have to admit I was a bit surprised. He was

M.L. Joslyn

larger than anyone I'd had. But he felt so good inside me. It could be that he knew how to use it, the way he had entered me with a certain gentle force, the way the ridge of the plump head had flicked at my clit, the way his inches had skated so easily to a depth I hadn't imagined possible. I had always thought such length, such thickness, would be, I mean—you know what I mean—right, ...Brooke?"

It wasn't the first time Amy had addressed either of the grad students by name. She wasn't sure if the informality pissed them off, but she didn't care. Maybe she'd get as personal with them as they'd been with her. She had aroused Brooke, had made her squirm, had caused her buttoned-down façade to crumble. They wanted to get personal? They got it. She waited for a response, any response.

"It's a common source of anxiety, Amy." Brooke cleared her throat before continuing, "It's quite normal to be apprehensive when trying something unfamiliar. This disquieting feeling can range from a mild unease to a full-on panic attack or even a sense of impending terror. Until we actually confront our fear and are able to separate fact from perception, we can't judge fairly. Yes, I know what you mean, Amy. Yes, I've had the same anxieties as you've had in your relationships. Am I good enough, pretty enough, smart enough? What does his cock look like, taste like ...feel like? Do I want him? Does he want me? Does he understand who I am? Will he want to have me ...forever?"

An easy quiet blanketed the room, like the thin wedge of silence that divided the stillness of night from the taunting light of dawn. Brooke had jumped off her pedestal, but it was too soon for any of them to see where she had landed.

Jeremy was unsure of where to go next, whether to proceed as if nothing had changed or to continue the string of revelations. He couldn't explain his state of mind to the girls. Not unless he was willing to explain himself to the dean later. Given the options, his choice was easy.

72

Chapter Nine

"Amy, which quality do you find most seductive in a sexual partner: a great body or a great personality?" Jeremy had scanned his list of potential questions, extracting the least provocative, closest-to-beige one he could find. He was but a few questions from disentangling himself from this spiraling mess, desperate for a shock of brisk afternoon air to fill his chest and slap him back to earth. He was hopeful, certain really, that Brooke was on the same page. Based on what he'd been witnessing, she'd be chilling her bones under a cold streaming shower the second she could find one, unless ...no, he wouldn't, couldn't allow himself to go there.

Anyway, there was only so much information he could squeeze from the alluring girl across the table before she'd crumble to a pile of nods and shrugs. It would be useless to keep pelting her with hardball questions. Besides, the harder he'd push, the more likely she'd be to start firing a few of her stinging, digressive rejoinders toward him instead of Brooke.

"How many questions have I answered for you guys?"

"You've been very forthcoming on a number of topics," Jeremy replied.

"Okay. So, have you learned anything about me yet?"

"We're not actually trying to learn about you, per se. We're just here to collect data. Your responses will be included in our study, along with the responses we receive from our other participants."

"I understand that. But that's not where I'm going with this, Jeremy. Do I seem shallow to you? Have I given you any reason to ask me that question?"

"It's just a question, Amy."

"Alright then. I guess the bottom line is, 'why would I give a shit about my sexual partner's personality?' Hey, if

M.L. Joslyn

he's hot and well-hung, why would I care if he's thoughtful or funny?"

"Amy," Brooke felt it necessary to break the awkward pause, "both Jeremy and I have learned a great deal from you, and about you, this afternoon. Sometimes a question such as the one Jeremy asked will reveal a well-cloaked belief you've yet to share. We don't know you that well yet."

"So, you plan on getting to know me better?" Amy watched Brooke as she fumbled for a response. Jeremy covered his mouth with his hand, as if trying to prevent renegade words from spilling forth.

Amy wondered how she could still be an enigma to Brooke and Jeremy. She'd shared so much of herself already, especially about Dylan. Maybe they hadn't heard her. Maybe they hadn't been paying attention. She was sure she had described Dylan's superficial attributes quite well. And she was pretty sure she'd talked about his personality, his thoughtfulness and his even disposition. Dylan was the most well balanced man she'd ever known: extremely good-looking with a boatload of sensitivity and kindness. She had mentioned that – right?

"We only have a few more questions for you, Amy," Jeremy answered, his voice skittish and brittle. "As much as we'd like to get to know you better, I'm not sure if there's time." Jeremy glanced at Brooke looking for a sign—any sort of sign.

"I'd like a new question then. I feel I've already answered the last one."

"Alright, Amy. How often do you fake your orgasm?" Jeremy considered it a matter-of-fact query that begged a simple, quantitative response. He wanted, needed to avoid another quicksand adventure.

"Shouldn't you ask if I've ever faked one first?"

Jeremy ran fingers through an imaginary goatee, contemplating his response. He took too long.

"I have a question," Brooke announced. "Amy, have you ever had group sex?"

The words flashed through Amy's ears as if they were on fire. She realized they'd leave an indelible scar if she didn't handle them carefully. Was Brooke headed somewhere with this? Or was it just another of her probing, intimate, whimsically- crafted personal questions.

"Once."

"Did you enjoy it?"

"Yes."

"Were you the only female in the group?"

"Yes."

"Why did you find it enjoyable?"

"Why? It was liberating. I was a goddess, at least for the evening. There were three of them, three friends of mine. They treated me ...very well."

"You were comfortable in that situation?"

"I was. I wouldn't have done it otherwise. We all knew it was a one-time thing."

"And you remained friends after?"

"Yeah. It wasn't strange for any of us, at least not at the time. We all loved each other, a sort of unconditional love, I'd say. It didn't affect our friendship after."

"Would you be open to having group sex again?"

"I'm not sure." Amy *was* certain, however, about Brooke, convinced now that she did want her—sexually. She wanted her and she wanted Jeremy too. He's in on it—he has to be, Amy thought. As if they weren't planning to get to know her better.

"So, it's something you might consider doing again?"

"It depends."

Jeremy wanted to call a time-out so he could huddle with Brooke, see if she were up to what he thought she was up to. But he couldn't. He didn't know her well enough to be so direct. Not when the circumstances were this delicate, this personal. He wasn't sure what his next step should be, but he knew he had to do something—soon.

Amy had been quite the little seductress all day, the way she talked, the way her legs begged Jeremy's contemplation, gesturing to him ...waving him in. And Brooke, alluring in an entirely different way, had him speculating, guessing. Who was she, really? And what did she want—from him—from Amy?

"Does it depend on the group, or does it depend on your needs?" Brooke asked.

The afternoon sun had shriveled toward evening's dusk, yet Jeremy's confusion failed to wilt with it. He needed to know things, but he wasn't allowed to ask. Why was Amy taunting him? *Because she could*, he decided. *And why had Brooke become so alluring?* He had no idea anymore who his colleague really was. He didn't even know what she really looked like. Somewhere under those wooly layers was a woman with a smart, perceptive mind, ambiguous heart, and selfishly smothered body.

"It's not something I think about, actually. Like I said, it happened once. It was the right time, with the right friends."

Jeremy wasn't just curious anymore. He *had* to know more about Brooke. He *had* to peek beneath those layers of pretense and layers of wool that concealed her truth so neatly. Hours earlier he had found her aloof, colorless, repellent even. Now he wished she would follow through on her cryptic threats, on her riddle-swathed promises, so he could see. He wanted her naked, metaphorically and physically. Maybe then she'd be revealed to him. Maybe then he'd see who she was, and he could determine whether his interest in her was anything more than a passing curiosity. *Come on, Brooke; strip down for us. You want us to see you, to know you. Do it, Brooke. Show us.*

"Amy," Jeremy paused, weakened by his thoughts, uncertain whether he should continue, "you've talked about your breasts, their influence on your behavior, their sway over your insecurities. We'd be interested to know if there are other drivers pressuring your behavior patterns."

"I don't understand. Other drivers?"

"Yes. Maybe there's something we can't see, something about you we wouldn't know unless you confided in us."

"Like some past trauma or something?"

"Possibly. But the way you've been presenting yourself to us this afternoon, your clenched legs juxtaposed against the coquettish hemline of your skirt, your self-doubt at odds with your intrepid sex life, make me think there's something else that you want to tell us about, something you subconsciously have a need to describe."

"Like what?"

"Your vagina, for instance."

"Seriously? How old are you—five? Here's an idea. You go first. Why don't you describe your cock for me? I mean, for us, right, Brooke?"

Brooke appeared unsettled by the exchange, her eyes racing to her iPad as if searching for the answer to ...anything. She waited, prayed for Jeremy to continue.

"Amy, it might help—us—and you. You've been very candid today. Brooke and I would be very appreciative if you could continue in that vein."

"What is it you want to hear, Jeremy? How much detail are you looking for? I don't have a problem with my pussy, if that's really what you're wondering. Maybe you're the one who has a problem with it. You want me to describe it? I can't. It looks different to me all the time. How about I show you, and you can describe it to me? Is that what you want? You want me to get naked for you? How about you, Brooke? You want to see my pussy too? You guys want to fuck me? You think your cock will satisfy me, Jeremy? You think I'd taste good, Brooke? Huh?"

"Amy, please," Jeremy mumbled.

M.L. Joslyn

"Please undress? Okay. Since you already know what my tits look like, I'll start by showing you my pussy."

"Amy, stop!" Jeremy's voice echoed off the walls, his words unambiguous and, with Amy's hands pulling at the hem of her skirt, justified. "I …you'll have to excuse me for a moment. All that coffee I drank earlier."

Jeremy dashed from the room while he had a chance, before either of the girls could question him or antagonize him further.

"I'm sure he'll be right back," Brooke announced, desperate for something to say.

"I don't doubt it," Amy replied, rushing the words from her throat. For the first time it was just the two of them in the room—three if counting the palpable caress of discomfort.

Amy wished Brooke and Jeremy would break down just as she had and lay their cards on the table. They had to realize the interview had become a hopeless mess and that they'd have nothing to lose at this point by being honest, not only with themselves, but also with her. They finally were all on the same page, weren't they? And they all wanted the same things, didn't they?

Brooke, on the other hand, was hopeful she could keep it together just a few more minutes. When Jeremy returned, she would announce that they'd collected enough responses from Amy. She was certain her partner would not disagree. They would thank the girl, pay her for her time, shake hands and smile politely. If all went well, she'd be home within the hour, free to reflect on her day, free to sort it into her fantasies—free to assign it a more fitting ending. She understood that the day might not have fallen to pieces if she had jumped from the stage as she'd wanted to and if she had stopped performing her patronizing, smarter-than-everyone routine—and if she'd been true to her feelings.

The glow caught a corner of Amy's vision, made her head turn just for a second. She looked back at Brooke, not wanting to share whatever, or whoever, was responsible for the sudden wink of light. This was Amy's distraction, not Brooke's. Brooke could stare out at the courtyard if she wanted, dreaming of springtime and hydrangeas and the promise of love; but she couldn't see what Amy could, beyond the courtyard and into another room. Amy's dreams weren't delusions. They were real enough to see, and close enough to direct with her thoughts.

Who was it this time? Amy wondered. Who was it that caused the light to glow on the other side of the tall sheets of glass and the tiny plot of embellished earth? Was it her TA, fresh from his shower, ready to signal his desire for her? Or was it someone else, someone new, someone who would find her as desirable as she might find him? She had to peek, but she wanted him for herself. Brooke could find her own lover for tonight. This one was Amy's—maybe. She had to see for herself.

"If we're waiting on Jeremy, I'm going to stretch my legs—if you don't mind."

"Sure, Amy. In fact, unless Jeremy has another question for you, we might even be done here. Go ahead, be comfortable."

Even better, Amy thought. She was free, her payday assured. She was no longer shackled to her chair, her personal life once again hers and hers alone. If she liked what she saw through the tall window, she wouldn't let him go, unless he …wasn't interested.

Amy stood, stretched and circled toward the rear of the room, carefully skirting the newcomer's field of vision. She would spy him before he could spy her, approve of him before he could reject her. She wouldn't hurt his feelings this way, not if he couldn't see her. He wouldn't notice her look of disapproval, or her beaming disappointment.

It was a man, for certain. There was no doubt in Amy's mind as she glanced from the edge of the tall pane. She made sure to keep him for herself by feigning exhaustion and showing disinterest. Brooke wouldn't think Amy was staring at anyone. She wouldn't know there was a man lurking about the room across the courtyard. It wouldn't even cross her mind.

Amy scrunched her eyes for a better look. With limited time to assess this man, she needed the extra focus. He approached the window, his window; and he became clearer. Amy watched him stretch, reaching for something, pulling at whatever it was. A curtain? Amy's room didn't have curtains; why did his? And why hadn't her TA used them, pulled them shut so she, so nobody, could see his unclothed body, his sleek, inviting body?

It was then that Amy recognized the man and understood his desire for privacy. He didn't want either of the girls across the courtyard to see that he had dodged them, that he had escaped the collapsing, backfiring probe into a certain female's sex life. He had distilled it to its essence, hadn't he, till it had been cornered, till it began to fight back.

Jeremy continued to pull on the curtain, nudging it carefully along the parched, unsympathetic rod from which it hung. The curtain seemed more fragile than the man prompting it, Amy decided. The material was apparently eggshell thin and withering, as if it had blanketed some other window for a long time and was then granted a second or last chance at usefulness. Jeremy stopped tugging when it could be pulled no further, when he had worked it closed to his satisfaction.

But it wasn't closed from Amy's perspective, not from the edge of the tall pane where she stood. She could still see him as he paced in a tight circle, hesitant about something, apparently struggling with invisible, demanding demons.

"I'm not sure what's taking him so long," Brooke said, breaking the leaden silence. "I suppose we could talk a bit till he returns. I don't know if I've properly thanked you for your contributions today, Amy."

"It's been interesting. I hope I've been helpful."

The silence returned, but Amy doubted that Jeremy would. He was still in the room across the courtyard, seated in the broad-armed chair that faced the window. He appeared uncomfortable, tortured even. With pangs of conscience stabbing at her heart, Amy thought about what she could do for him. She was no longer certain of what she had done *to* him.

Her uncertainty was erased when she noticed he'd resolved his struggle, had made up his own mind, for better or worse. With his head back, pressed into the dense seat cushion as if preparing for takeoff, he reached for his crotch. He grabbed at it verifying all was as it should be or where it should be—Amy wasn't sure which. He palmed the area and then began to fondle himself. She could see him clearly, or clearly enough, to spy the outline of his erection. It pressed with urgency inside his incarcerating slacks, lengthening at a relentless pace as his fingers and his imagination worked their magic.

Jeremy stopped touching himself and slouched in the chair, his engorged prick casting a clear, formidable profile, easily understood and appreciated from the room across the courtyard.

But he wasn't finished. He hadn't even started, really. With a flick of his wrist, Jeremy had his zipper down, exhaling as his nimble fingers disappeared through the space he'd created. A grin crossed Amy's face as she watched his thick pole spring through the opening. Her smile was in part a consequence of his cock lurching to attention; she could almost hear the *boinggg* as it flicked from his trousers, as if she were watching a scene from a pornographic cartoon.

But she was also smiling because she liked what she saw. His erection was stiff, large—but not unmanageable—and nicely defined by its unswerving lines and clit-nudging ridges. It was just the type Amy enjoyed contemplating, just the type she liked to scrutinize when pulsing thick streams of milky come would shoot from its tip and spread across innocent, aimless trails.

Amy stayed focused on Jeremy's prick, anxious for his next move; would he be timid with it, would he toy with it or would he smother it with his fist to hasten his release? She was sure he wouldn't be clumsy with it—not Jeremy—not the man who spent his days composing the quintessential almanac of sex.

Curiously he didn't seem in much of a hurry. But he didn't seem too cautious either. Jeremy gripped his cock with intent and started stroking at a restrained, indulging pace, not with the expected flurry of jerks and punches. He wasn't pleading for his orgasm—he was encouraging it. He didn't seem to hate himself for the state he was in—he seemed to be ...loving himself.

"This is disturbing," Brooke declared while parking her iPad on the squat table by her knees. "It's unacceptable. I apologize for this."

Amy was startled by Brooke's disclosure. She was certain that Jeremy had been doing himself out of Brooke's line of sight; she guessed she'd been wrong about that. Then she realized that she'd been busted as well and wondered if Brooke deemed her a pervert for watching him, or if she simply considered her a curious voyeur. Amy wasn't embarrassed, though she did feel for Jeremy. The guy just needed to get himself off. Perhaps it wasn't the best time or the best place for such a thing, she supposed, but he had to do what he had to do.

"It's really no big deal, Brooke. I can wait for him to finish."

"How long could it possibly take him?" Brooke replied. "I bet I know what happened. I bet he ran into a colleague of his, or perhaps one of his students, and he's unable to wrangle himself away from the conversation. Let me go find him, Amy. I'll bring him back right away and we can wrap this up. Thank you again for being so patient."

"Oh, believe me, Brooke. I'm happy to wait. I bet you're right. I bet he's been coerced into some unavoidable situation. I appreciate your going to search for him. Good luck!"

"Thanks Amy. I'll return shortly, one way or another."

Chapter Ten

Five minutes. That's how long Brooke had been searching for Jeremy, and she wasn't about to waste a minute more. The man had deserted her for the day—and possibly forever. If he had made the choice to abandon their jointly contrived study and head for higher ground, there was little Brooke could do to stop him. Better now than later, she thought.

Amy was the first of many participants to sit for this study. If Brooke had done her homework on the girl, maybe spent a few more minutes with her when she had signed her up, she'd have scheduled her to be last, not first. Brooke knew from experience that the others wouldn't be like Amy. Odds were they'd be more apprehensive, more skittish, less explicit and less seductive. And odds were Jeremy would still be onboard, unfazed by the predictably pedestrian process.

Instead, the wrong girl, or the best girl if her rich contributions meant anything, went first and spoiled the whole thing.

All Brooke wanted to do now was go home and deal with her stifled cravings in an un-businesslike manner, away from the restrictions of her position and away from campus. She'd thank Amy the moment she returned to the room, hand her an envelope of cash, and send her on her way.

"Amy!"

The voice was clear, and it belonged to Jeremy. Brooke must have missed him, possibly passed him in the hallway, unaware, her mind someplace else.

"That's right, Amy! That's perfect!"

Where were they? Brooke wondered. What was she doing to him? Or worse, what was he doing to her?

Brooke regained focus as she picked up her pace.

Jeremy's voice was too close. This is not where she'd left Amy; she was down the next hallway. At least that's where she'd left her. Amy must have gone on her own search for Jeremy, and she must have found him.

"No, leave the skirt on, Amy."

Jeremy's voice was more restrained, more discreet. Mixed emotions flooded Brooke's head. She wanted to find him, to stop him from doing something he would regret later. But she didn't want to find *them*, nor did she want to see *them*. Leave the skirt on? There was no doubt in Brooke's mind what they were up to. Still, she didn't want to know. At least that's what she kept telling herself.

Brooke edged toward Jeremy's voice, slipping past one empty room and then another. She was certain he was in one of the three faculty lounges that flanked one side of the hallway. It must be this one, she thought. *Go ahead, Jeremy, tell Amy what you want. Let me hear you plead. Let me hear her moan. And, and ...let me in. I won't say a word, and I won't interfere—unless you want me to.*

"This is how I like it, Amy. Is this how you like it?"

Brooke stood outside the door, waiting for Amy's response. They must be fucking, Brooke assumed. Amy wasn't uttering a word, so she must be busy with ...something. Brooke pressed closer, hoping to catch a sound, any sound. A couple of muted sighs, that was all she could distinguish. She wasn't certain if it were Amy expressing her pleasure or Jeremy voicing his.

"It's okay, Brooke. You can join us now. Come on, let's see what you've got."

Brooke backed away from the door, confused, embarrassed—busted. They must have heard her bump against the wall or rattle the door as she embraced it with her ear. And now Jeremy was calling for her, wanting her to join them. Could he persuade her to have sex with them? What should she do? She couldn't think about this. She thought too much about too many things. She was still young. She was still a student. Remember this day, Brooke told herself. It's only once. This will never happen again.

"Sure, Jeremy. I'll show you what I've …"

They scrutinized one another for a second, assembling their thoughts, their responses. Brooke had already thrown her blazer to the floor and her heart to the hurricane of breaths that swirled through the room. Her fingers had already pushed open half the buttons to her bright pink blouse. She had never felt more exposed than she did at that moment. A naked man was an arm's length away, pumping his thick hard-on with two hands, yet she was the one fumbling for a grain of composure. She was the one who was fearful of rejection.

"Brooke. Don't stop, Brooke. Your blouse …"

Brooke didn't know how to respond. She wasn't sure what she should do. Jeremy didn't seem a bit unnerved by the interruption. He continued to masturbate as if stopping were the last thing on his mind. She didn't want him to stop either, but she couldn't continue to gawk. She *could* button up and turn around; the door was right behind her. But there were things she wanted to see, to feel, to experience, like his lean, strong body, his beautifully enlightened mind and his long, hard cock.

"It's *you*, Brooke. I want *you*."

"That's not true. Someone else is responsible for this, for us behaving this way."

"Come here. Don't touch that blouse. Let me …"

"You want her, I know. I'm convenient, that's all."

Jeremy let his hands fall to the bent leather of his perch. His erection hadn't lost an ounce of energy, throbbing along with his heart. "She is very …seductive, isn't she?"

Brooke wasn't sure how to respond. For maybe the first time in her life, she wasn't sure about anything. "I suppose she is."

"She's interesting, isn't she? A plaything perhaps? But it's you, Brooke. I want to get to know *you* better. Come here—please?"

"Not while you're thinking of her."

"It works both ways, Brooke."

"What do you mean?"

"You want her too, don't you? You can't stop thinking about her. You can't help but wonder."

"But I think you and I would make ..."

"Shhh ...I think so too. Come here."

***

Amy was incredulous as she gazed across the narrow courtyard. How could they be so oblivious? she wondered. She did appreciate a good show, and Brooke and Jeremy did not disappoint. But, after ten minutes of watching, she thought it was time for her to leave. If it weren't for the tidy envelope of cash she had earned but had yet to receive, she would have already bolted. She'd had her fill and it was time. She'd stop by tomorrow for her payday. She was fine with that.

As she bent to retrieve her purse, Amy's phone chirped for attention. It was another text from Dylan. *"Can you talk?"*

Amy stuffed her phone back in her purse. Yeah, she would talk to him; as soon as she was out of the building, she'd call. She'd sip from the crisp, early evening air while strolling the tangle of pathways across the Oval, phone tight to her ear.

But Dylan couldn't wait that long. Amy's phone rang while she was stealing one final glance into the room across the way.

"Hey."

"Sorry, Amy. I needed to talk to you. Are you still in your interview?"

M.L. Joslyn

"No. What's up? How's the party?"

"I left. Listen, I had no idea you were interviewing. I want to hear all about it. But I need to get something off my chest first. Do you have a minute?"

"I guess," Amy replied, chewing over her likely reaction to his forthcoming confession.

"I've been interviewing too. I didn't want to say anything until I got an offer. I haven't gotten one, an offer that is, but I'm not giving up. I want to stay in Columbus another year, until you graduate. If you're good with that, I guess."

"Why wouldn't you tell me about this? What were you afraid of?"

"Failure, rejection—I don't know. This job search has really been stressing me out, Amy. I'm about to graduate, yet I can't find a job. I've had six interviews with six different firms. That's six companies that don't want me. I'm not done though. If I need to intern somewhere to get started, that's what I'll do. Unless you'd rather I …"

"Dylan, I need to go. I'll call you back in a little bit. Promise."

Amy almost dropped her phone when she heard the rasping sweep of an opening door. Flushed faces streaked by crowing optimism greeted her startled gaze.

"Amy, glad you're still here."

Amy almost didn't recognize Brooke's voice. It was softer, mellower, conversational. Jeremy seemed as if he couldn't speak, even if he'd wanted to.

"I was about to leave actually."

"I would have felt horrible if you had. Here, your reward for withstanding our …interrogation—two hundred cash."

"Thanks. It was an interesting day: pretty cathartic, very interesting."

"Could I, could we—sorry, Jeremy—ask you one more thing?"

"Why not? But could I ask you something first?"

"Sure. Go ahead."

"You two had never fucked before, had you?"

Brooke walked to the far window and gazed, as if she were dreaming, across the courtyard. "No. We hadn't."

"Just checking. What did you want to ask me?"

"Would you ever cheat on your boyfriend?"

Amy turned toward Jeremy, his eyes hopeful but undemanding. "No. No, I wouldn't."

"Okay." Brooke looked out the window before continuing, "Thank you so much for your time, Amy. You've been extremely helpful."

"So have you, Brooke. So have you."

The End